# Child of Spring

*For Basanta.*
*For Mumma, with eternal love and honor.*
—F. Z.

Jennifer Unter, Kathy Landwehr, and
Vicky Holifield, you helped make it possible. Thank you!

Published by
PEACHTREE PUBLISHERS
1700 Chattahoochee Avenue
Atlanta, Georgia 30318-2112
*www.peachtree-online.com*

Text © 2016 by Farhana Zia
Cover and interior illustrations © 2016 Adela Pons

Design and composition by Nicola Carmack and Melanie Ives

Printed in January 2016 in Harrisonburg, Virginia, by RR Donnelley & Sons
10 9 8 7 6 5 4 3 2 1
First Edition

Library of Congress Cataloging-in-Publication Data

Names: Zia, F. (Farhana)
Title: Child of spring / Farhana Zia.
ISBN 978-1-56145-904-9
Description: Atlanta : Peachtree Publishers, [2016. | Summary: In India, young Basanta struggles to accept her role as servant to a temperamental rich girl while dreaming of having a beautiful ring of her own.
Identifiers: LCCN 2015014790
Subjects: | CYAC: Social classes—Fiction. | Family life—India—Fiction. | Friendship—Fiction. | India—Fiction.
Classification: LCC PZ7.Z482 Chi 2016 | DDC [Fic]—dc23

LC record available at *http://lccn.loc.gov/2015014790*

# Child of Spring

## Farhana Zia

**PEACHTREE**
ATLANTA

*O*ld Nahni, who was my dear grandmother, used to tell me that I was named after the happy spring season in which I was born. "Don't you know, Basanta," she would say, "some of the gladness that came from the birds and flowers rubbed right off on your little infant heart?"

My grandmother said that on the day I was born, the sky celebrated with green, purple, and yellow kites soaring and dipping majestically. Every year, when the kites appeared in the sky, I made her tell my story again and again, until her tongue clacked on her teeth.

"You were born before summer sizzled," she told me. "That day the air was cool and the grass was lush."

"Tell me…were there gifts for me?" I asked one year, but Old Nahni shook her head. "Na," she said, "but there was a lot of singing of songs and clapping of hands in the hut."

"Singing and clapping are not as nice as the gifts wrapped in colorful paper that my mistress Little Bibi gets," I grumbled, but my grandmother only chucked me under the chin and said, "A song from the heart is more golden than a nicely wrapped gift, my child of spring."

"A ring with shiny stones like the one on Little Bibi's finger would make a nice present," I sighed.

"Wish and wish on it, my own child of spring," Old Nahni said, "and a queen of fairies will bring it someday."

But how, oh how, could I hope for a fairy to grant my wish? And how, oh how, could a song from the heart be better than a real present?

# Chapter 1

Yesterday Little Bibi practically called me a thief. I got so mad at my mistress that I was ready to spit, but I didn't dare. My ears burned, and there was a tickle in my nose. I bungled all my duties that morning. When I poured water into her glass, I sloshed it on the table. When I slapped at the mosquitoes in her bedding net, I missed again and again.

"Keep your mind on your work, *na*!" chided my mother, but how could I?

The rest of the day at the Big House didn't go well, and I was still upset that evening. When the next morning came and it was time to get up and go to work, I wanted to hide myself away in our little hut. But there was no place to hide, so I burrowed into my mother's lap and cried a river.

"I quit!" I sobbed. "Please, Amma, please. I don't want to report to work today!"

But the words got all muffled up inside the cottony folds of her sari. Amma clucked her tongue. "*Aiyyo!* What are you muttering?" she asked.

The impatience in my mother's voice was not a good

sign. I lifted my head and tried to get her attention. "Please, Amma, please!"

I didn't want to be a servant girl in the Big House anymore—not today, not ever! I didn't want to walk barefoot on a long pebbly road, just to sweep and fetch and carry and answer, "Yes, Little Bibi. Right away, Little Bibi." I didn't want to gather eggs from the henhouse for her breakfast omelet, which Amma always cooked with a sprinkle of green chili and a sprig of garden-fresh coriander.

Normally, being Amma's helper in the Big House wasn't so bad. The sofas were velvety and soft, the carpets spread out like fields of flowers, and cooling fans twirled on the high ceilings. In the courtyard, sweet-smelling motia bushes blossomed and roosters roamed. Fish swam in a lily-covered pond and the garden was dazzling with its bougainvillea vines and hibiscus bushes.

It also helped that Amma and I had a system to keep me out of trouble with my young mistress on the harder days. "Mind! She blows hot today," Amma would whisper to me, and armed with caution, I'd step gingerly out of Little Bibi's path.

My young mistress was an unpredictable girl. On good days, she was as sweet as the spring breeze and gave me her old dolls. Sometimes for *Divali*, she even gave me small gifts wrapped in brown paper. But on the bad days, when she was as fiery as a mango pickle, she stomped and screamed for no good reason. And yesterday she had been in a particularly rotten mood.

"Amma!" I cried. "Little Bibi says I am a thief!"

"Come, come. She didn't actually say 'thief.'" Amma's fingers fluttered over my hair, which was so tightly braided that it pulled the skin on my neck.

Early morning was the wrong time to bend Amma's ear. There were many things to do before the long walk to the Big House. My father's milky tea was boiling over on the woodstove, and my baby sister Durga needed feeding too.

"But Amma, she didn't have to! She said her precious ring disappeared from her room and then she looked at me!"

"She only looked," my mother reminded me.

"With such angry eyes!"

*"Arrey daiyya!"* My mother nudged my head off her lap. "Little Bibi was probably distraught."

"I don't know anything about her ring." I sniffled. "I would have said so if I did."

If I had seen the ring, I surely would have told her. "Little Bibi, look!" I would have said. "Here's your beautiful ring and I have found it for you!" I would have done that even though seeing the red and white stones sparkle against my own brown finger would be the best dream come true, and even though Little Bibi had so many nice things that one less hardly made a difference.

"It'll get found," Amma said absently. She shuffled around on her haunches under our low, low ceiling, packing roti for my father's lunch in his tiered tiffin box. That was a signal for me to get on with the day. It was no use. There was no getting out of working at the Big House today. I would have to face Little Bibi and her accusing eyes whether I wanted to or not.

"I'm going to the tamarind tree!" I declared. Under my favorite tree I could sit and think and no one would shout orders at me.

Amma looked at me askance. "Off to dawdle and daydream under that tree again?"

"I'm not going to dawdle and I am not going to daydream!" I said. "I'm going to see Dinoo Kaka. He is my very good friend, you know."

"You've spent far too much time with that crow," Amma said. "He has surely flown his nest by now anyway."

"*Na!* He waits for me and he pays attention when I have something important to say!" I grabbed my doll Tikki and snatched a scrap of bread from my breakfast plate.

"Keep the bread for yourself and let the crow eat from the garbage bins!" Amma shouted.

I ignored her and ducked out of our smoky hut and into the fresh air. The beaten earth was hard underfoot. A spring breeze rippled my skirt and rustled the leaves in the guava tree. I breathed deeply. The air was light and the sweet smell of a flower filled my nose.

I heard Dinoo Kaka cawing in the distance, so I zigzagged quickly through the maze of mud and straw huts that sat silent and shadowy in the awakening light.

I brushed past the broom that belonged to the betel-nut-leaf seller and skirted around the bangle woman's basket. The knife grinder's stone stood silently by his hut, and an elephant ear shaped rice winnow made of woven palm frond lay upturned by the old cobbler's door. The chickens belonging to Rukmani, his daughter, squawked at me as if they were passing on an unpleasant message. Rukmani, a girl with a scheming mind and a sharp tongue, never wasted a chance to put me in my place. I leaped over the *rangoli* pattern near the washerwoman's door, careful not to disturb the pretty red and white swirls she drew on the earth each morning.

Lali's home lay ten steps away, but I didn't call for her. I knew she was still asleep behind the limp curtain that hung in the doorway. She'd be up soon enough to take charge while her mother was at work.

Amma says that Lali and I are like two wings of a butterfly, each one fluttering with the other in perfect harmony. Just two years older than I, Lali was my best friend. If she knew about Little Bibi's accusation, she'd put her arm around my neck and cluck her tongue and say she understood. I would tell her everything on my way back home.

The garbage bins were spilling over and I pinched my nose. Then I let go and took a deep breath when I passed the water pump, where the air was humid and the smells were refreshingly damp and clean.

The tamarind tree loomed ahead, strong and erect like a turbaned soldier standing guard atop the little knoll. Behind it, the sky was changing from red to saffron to pink. I heard green pods rustling in the fern-like leaves above. I ran up, sank to the earth with my back against the broad trunk, and put the piece of bread on the ground beside me.

Dinoo Kaka swooped down with a flurry and a flap. He pecked and jabbed at the bread, and it disappeared before I could count to ten. Then he cocked his head at me.

"Sorry." I showed him my empty hands. "You'll have to wait till tomorrow."

I'd bring him a more generous piece the next day if Amma didn't grumble too much. But tomorrow was a long time away and there was still today to worry about.

It was going to be a long day at the Big House—a day filled with brooms and dustcloths and washrags; a day stacked with rumpled beds and dirty plates; a day overflowing with Memsaab's calls of "Basanta, do this, do that! Basanta, fetch this, fetch that!"

But worst of all, it would be another day filled with Little Bibi.

How could Amma be so unbending? She had such firm notions about the rightness of things and the wrongness of things, and missing even one day at work fell squarely on the wrong side of the line. She never looked at things from my side. It was not fair!

"Amma's not being helpful. She's going to call me any

minute now, just you wait and see!" I told Dinoo Kaka.

"*Caw, caw?*"

Somehow I didn't find any comfort in the crow's response this morning. I sang a lullaby to Tikki to distract myself—a soft song my grandmother used to sing to calm me at night when I was a little girl. "*Ooo-hai-gay, ooo-hai-ma…*"

Slap, slap, my leg beat on the earth and Tikki bounced in my lap.

Poor little thing! My doll was bedraggled now, and too old to do anything except lie still. Her big brown eyes never closed, and her dress hid a hole in her middle. When Little Bibi first gave her to me, Tikki's cheeks were the color of a rose petal, but now they were smudged and a voice that had once sweetly called out *Mama* was lost.

Still, she always made a pretty bride when I wed her to Lali's Dear Boy. We had celebrated five weddings already, even as Amma grumbled that we were getting much too old for dolls and Lali was nearly old enough to start thinking about her own wedding!

How could that be? How could one be too old for fun?

"*Ooo-hai-gay, ooo-hai-ma.*" I closed my eyes and waited for the magic that changed me instantly from a poor girl in a little hut to a rich girl in a Big House to happen. But it didn't. Not today.

The tamarind tree was my private nest, a place where all my secret dreams came to pass. Usually all I needed to do was close my eyes, think hard, and *poof!* there I was, in my very own room, with my very own plump pillow, on my very own soft bed. A ring brighter than a full moon sparkled on my finger—a ring that was mine not because I stole it, but because Bapu bought it for me from Zaveri's Pearl and Gold Shop, because he promised he would, and he always kept his word.

But there was no luxurious room for me today, and when my mind drifted to the ring, I was brought back to the present with a heavy heart.

Dinoo Kaka hopped around for a while longer, and then he gave up and flew away.

The sun was climbing in the sky, burning away dawn's dim light. I sensed the furrows in Amma's brows deepening, but I didn't want to return home yet. I was not ready for the long walk to the Big House, and I was not ready to face Little Bibi's accusing eyes.

But just as I feared, Amma's voice echoed through the thatched huts, curved around the guava tree, flew past the garbage bins and the water pump, and came for me.

"Basanta!"

*Aiyyo!* I didn't want to go. But Amma called again, and now her voice was hard. The ring was missing and Little Bibi thought I took it. I was *not* Rukmani, the old cobbler's daughter who made lovely clay pots but was also a liar and a thief. I was a decent girl, an upright and honest girl. I was Amma's child.

Amma had called, and there was nothing to do but obey.

# Chapter 2

The station tower clock struck seven times. One by one, the residents of my *busti* ducked out of their huts. Bangles jangled on the women's wrists. The men puffed on their cheroots and coiled long strips of turban cloth around their heads.

The line at the water pump was already getting long and Rukmani was at the front of it, filling her pretty clay pots. I ducked my head and walked by quietly. I didn't want to be peppered with questions about life at the Big House: "How many fluffy pillows on Little Bibi's bed, *hanh*? How many ribbons for Little Bibi's hair? How many eggs on Little Bibi's breakfast plate? Come, tell me, *nai*?"

But before I could slip away, Rukmani stretched her long swan neck in my direction. *"Arri,* Basanta," she called. "Why are you sneaking away? And why such a long face, *hanh*?"

I dodged the chickens and broke into a fast trot, my bare feet slapping hard against the earth.

"Did the old crow fly away with your tongue?" she called after me.

That Rukmani! *Her* tongue was like a cobra's. *Pfft!* Her words lashed out and left prickly stings on my back.

I wound around the mango tree and skipped over a goat's tether. Then I turned the corner and made for Lali's hut, hoping she'd be awake by now. When I saw dust billowing at her door, I called out, "Lali, oh Lali!" She stopped sweeping, straightened up, and tucked a strand of hair behind her ear. "What?"

"Throw down your broom. I have something to tell, and I am in the mood for a quick game of Seven Tiles too."

"Seven Tiles at this hour? Have you gone mad?" Lali twirled her finger beside her head. "I have a pile of work to finish before the little ones wake up. Besides, didn't your mother just call for you?" She flicked the tip of her broom to loosen a chicken feather.

"Yeah, yeah!" I sat on my haunches. "Did Vimla Mausi leave already?"

Lali nodded. Her mother, whom I called *mausi*, even though she wasn't really my auntie, was already at work sweeping the streets and Lali was in charge of her family for the day.

"I wouldn't mind a day off," I sighed. "It's very hard work at the Big House."

Lali arched one eyebrow.

"Oh, I know what you're thinking," I said. "And you can stop thinking it!"

Yes, Lali knew all about the Big House, because she had heard me go on and on about it. But she only remembered the good parts—the crystal chandelier far lovelier than a night sky, and the China rug more beautiful than a rose garden. She knew about the bougainvillea vines that spilled bloodred flowers and the fish that swam round and round in a quiet pond. What a perfect fairyland the Big House was! How hard could it be to work in it? This is what she was thinking! She was not thinking about the stacks of dirty dishes and the piles of rumpled sheets!

"A big house makes very big work, Lali. I've told you one hundred times. My work is much harder than this." I swept my hand to indicate the hut and the patch of dirt outside, all nice and tidy as a result of my friend's diligent broom.

"Go, go!" Lali said. "I wouldn't mind fluffing up soft pillows so very much. And I wouldn't mind serving food at a table so shiny you could see your face smiling right back at you."

"You'd mind it if your mistress screamed at you and called you by a very bad name, though, wouldn't you?" I asked.

"What did she say exactly? Did she use a swear word?"

"She may as well have. She thinks I stole her ring and she practically called me a thief!"

"*Oo Maa!*" Lali clamped a hand to her mouth. "She called you *that*? How dare she?"

"I didn't take it. I wouldn't!"

"I know! I know!" Lali traced an arc in the dust with her left foot—the bad one that made her limp when she

13

walked. For the longest time she didn't say anything.

"What are you thinking?" I prodded.

"I am thinking…that if you had found it, you would have returned it. Because if you hadn't your Little Bibi would surely pack you off to the police *thaana, nai?*"

"*Daiyya re daiyya!*" I exclaimed. "Prisons are for thieves which I surely am not. I told you I didn't know anything about it!"

"I am also thinking," Lali continued, "that maybe the ring *will* be found and Little Bibi will be so very happy. *Oo Maa!* Thinking about this is making me think of other happy things."

"What other happy things?"

"That we should arrange another wedding between Dear Boy and Tikki sooner rather than later."

I clapped my hands. I was glad to change the subject. A wedding celebration would be just the thing to take my mind off Little Bibi. We'd invite Lali's siblings, Nandi, Pummi, Dev, and Hari. Lali would want Ganga the Milk Boy there too. Why, we could even invite Bala!

"I'll put it in Amma's ear," I said. "She'll be difficult at first but she'll give in by and by."

Lali nodded. "Don't worry. Your mother will be as sweet as a sugar crystal and let us have some sticky lentil balls for the wedding feast. Just you wait and see!"

We sat down side by side, leaned against the mud wall, and stretched out our legs. A breeze carried the scent of flowers to my nose yet again.

"My father says that the roses are preparing to bloom in the Public Gardens," I said. He sometimes brought home a handful of yellow and white flowers for Amma's prayer altar.

Lali's hand went to her ear and I noticed the little yellow flower tucked behind it.

"Hello? What's this?" I asked.

"It's nothing." She dropped her hand quickly into her lap, her face turning a deeper color.

"It's not *nothing*," I retorted. "Where did you get it? Tell me!"

Lali suddenly got all squirmy. "From a bush that grows by the riverbank."

"You went to the riverbank without me?"

"Kites are going to fly soon, I bet!" She pointed skyward, trying to distract me.

The wily thing had changed the subject deftly, but she was right about the kites. Flowers meant spring, and spring was the time for paper kites to skitter and soar like rainbow-colored insects.

Spring was also a proper time for a birthday party, but such celebrations skipped my hut year after year. Birthdays were for Big Houses. I only got a kiss on the brow.

I gazed skyward. Thinking about the kites reminded me of the luscious colors in Little Bibi's birthday cakes. But when I thought of the kites dipping, rising, and twirling through the sky, it moved my mind to other things.

"I'm placing my bets on Bala again. He had better not

let me down this time," I said. I had lost a pile of tamarind seeds when Paki had won the championship last year, beating Bala by a very narrow margin.

"*Oo Maa!*" Lali poked me in the shoulder in a teasing way.

"Don't be an idiot!" I said. "He's just a crazy boy of the street, who happens to be a master kite flyer. He got a tiny bit unlucky because Paki cheated."

"And who just also happens to think you're a spitfire *Divali* firecracker!"

"That's not true!" I snapped.

"And who runs about saying your teeth are as shiny as pearls!"

I shoved Lali roughly away, but she swayed right back. "I swear it on my mother!" she said with a big grin.

"Bala is a pest!" I retorted. "And if you're going to be an idiot, I have no time for you either!" I got up and started to walk away.

"The boy is absolutely gaga for you!" Lali bubbled. "God promise!"

I turned around and stuck my tongue out at her, then flicked a thumb against my chin for good measure.

# Chapter 3

I raised the jute flap on our door and let my eyes readjust to the dimness of the close quarters. How small my hut was! Ten strides, and I could travel from this end to the far one. Why, Little Bibi's eating table seemed bigger than our home!

Smoke rose from the hearth. It mingled with the first rays of sunlight that streamed through a small opening high up in the wall. Smoke in the daytime, smoke at night—*Arrey daiyya!* But without the smoking hearth, there would be no fire, and without a fire there would be no milky tea in the morning nor steaming rice at night. Without a smoky fire to cook them, the lentils would stay in the bag to be nibbled up by mice, and the spices and tamarind would be of no use at all.

I had a suspicion the cockroach was secretly stirring his antennae behind the kindling pile. Closer to the hearth, brass pots were stacked on shelves, the coconut shell ladle lay in the water pot, and the palm frond mat was smooth underfoot. The Big Box was well hidden under my father's cot. "Talk to no one about it," Amma had warned me time and again. Inside it were all of our nice things, safely tucked away.

Amma had promised that she would prepare a respectable trousseau for me, one pretty piece at a time, and it would all go into the Big Box to wait until I had my own wedding. "What will it be?" I'd asked her, fingering a small piece of wood in one corner of the box. If you pulled hard enough on the chip, it lifted to reveal a hollow, the size of a quail egg, in the wooden base.

"Something nice to put around your dainty ankles," Amma told me.

My father's chai tea smelled of cinnamon and cloves. I walked over for my usual sip. "I want to stay home today, Bapu," I whispered in his ear. "May I?"

"*Na*, little one." Bapu shook his head, then tipped tea from his cup into his saucer for me.

In the little mirror that hung on the wall, I could see Amma's reflection. She stared at me while she placed the customary *bindi*, a big vermilion dot, in the middle of her forehead with her middle finger. My mother was ready now. Her hair was coiled in a tight bun, the red dot glistened on her forehead like a third eye, and her sari was hitched up around her ankles. "Let's go!" she commanded, swooping Durga up in her arms. "Hurry! Hurry!"

I scrambled out after her.

A large field sprawled between the huts and the long road that led to the Big House. In the summertime, the ground was as dry as a chicken bone and as dusty as ground spice, but during the rainy season, it became lush green and spongy underfoot.

Amma's toe rings rang sharply against the pebbles, and dust rose around her feet. *"Juldi! Juldi!"* she urged. "Walk faster!"

In a few minutes we reached the far end of the field, where it met the road and the jamun tree rained down fat berries that splattered the ground with purple. More often than not, Paki and Raju, the washerwoman's sons, perched in it overhead, spitting seeds at passersby. I peered up into the tree, but today it was empty.

Amma noticed this too. "I wonder what mischief those naughty fellows are wreaking."

Everyone had learned to look out for Paki and Raju. They always had our *busti* in an uproar: breaking a pot here, untying the goat's tether there, pouring mud in the cobbler's shoes, chucking mango seeds at chickens.

"Why can't they be more like Ganga?" Amma grumbled. "Now there's a lad who makes his father proud!"

Ganga the Milk Boy might well be good and friendly, but Paki and Raju were far more interesting. "Ganga is a wet rag," I said. "He's nothing more than a stuttering simpleton."

My mother looked at me so hard that I had to lower

my eyes. I didn't look up until we reached the end of the beaten path through the field.

It was still too early in the day for the road to roar like a lion, but it had begun to purr like a house cat. Bicycles, rickshaws, and bullock carts weaved in and out of each other's paths. Pushcarts filled with colorful fruits and vegetables rattled along. The peanut man passed us, a basket balanced atop his head and a cane stand tucked in his armpit. The knife grinder was out and about with his stone, ready for business.

The asphalt surface felt different underfoot, harder and grainier than packed earth and more scalding in the summer. Just ahead, a mica wafer glinted in the road, too large to ignore.

I snatched it and held it up to the sunlight. "Look how this one shines!" It was a beautiful specimen, the best and biggest one I had found so far, the color of weakest tea, and without an imperfection anywhere. It was so translucent that I could see the lines in my hand through it. "I am putting it in my treasure box as soon as we get home."

But Amma only shifted Durga's weight from one hip to the other and hurried me on. "Walk faster! We have no time for trinkets in the road."

"What's the hurry?" I muttered. "Lalla-ji's grain store hasn't even opened for business yet. I seriously doubt that we are going to be late." I put the mica away in my pocket.

# Child of Spring

We continued walking at a good clip, passing dilapidated shacks and ramshackle storefronts. Metal doors rolled up with loud rattles and shopkeepers shouted morning greetings. And then I spied Bala shooting marbles on the other side of the road.

"*Tcha*! Rolling marbles again!" Amma grumbled. "I've told that boy one hundred times to find an honorable job for a decent wage."

"I don't know why you worry about him so much," I said. "You're not even his mother!"

My mother had a special liking for Bala. "What brilliant eyes the boy has in his head!" she had remarked. "And look at the shape and size of his forehead!" According to her, these things were signs of great intelligence. She had even pleaded his case to Memsaab, hoping she could find him a position, but the mistress already had her cook and gardener and chauffeur, and her other *memsaab* friends weren't hiring either. Still, Amma didn't let up.

Bala saw us coming. He whistled so loud, I practically jumped out of my skin.

"What?" I asked.

"Watch this!" he yelled.

I stopped to look. I couldn't help it. Bala *was* clever!

He squinted and aimed and, true to form, the marble struck its target. Then it ricocheted sharply, missing a drain hole by a hair. If the marble had curved even the slightest bit more to the right, Bala's marble would have slid down,

Farhana Zia

down, down with all the rainwater, all the way to *Inglistan*. Little Bibi said *Inglistan* was on the other side of the world, where the queen lived with the Kohinoor diamond fixed in the middle of her crown.

"*Arrey wah!*" Bala's victory yell rang out on the morning air.

"Just a fluke! Just a fluke!" I shouted back.

Bala scooped up his marbles and deftly dodged motor-cars and bullock carts to get to our side of the road. "Hold up!" he panted. He sounded like Kalu the mangy dog that hangs around looking for food. "Tell me, oh do—did you miss me between yesterday and today?"

"Go! Go!" I waved him back.

What a stupid owl he was! How dare he think such a ridiculous thing? Was I even the tiniest bit like Rukmani, batting my eyes at boys? *Na!* I had better things to do with my time than waste it thinking about him.

"No need to get all riled up," Amma said. "The boy is only playing with you."

"Lali said your precious boy got a thrashing for stealing peanuts yesterday," I told her. "Did you know that, *hanh*?"

"Lali's a liar!" Bala shouted.

Amma ruffled his hair. "Tell me what happened then."

Bala shrugged. "There was no beating, Yella Mausi. How could there be? I ran away like the wind."

"*Aiyyo.* Why did you dip your hand in the man's basket?"

Bala hung his head. "I...I was hungry," he mumbled.

22

Amma's voice softened and the furrows in her forehead flattened out. "There are better ways, dear boy."

"I urgently wanted something to eat," Bala said. "I toss and turn on my mat when I am hungry." He rattled the marbles in his fist and turned away from her.

"*Tch-tch. Aiyyo!*"

I stiffened. How could my mother be one way with me and another with Bala? She was all "*Tch-tch*" and "*Aiyyo*" for Bala, but for me it was "Hurry up!" or "Stop daydreaming!" She understood the stolen peanuts but she didn't understand Little Bibi's accusing voice. It was not fair!

Amma placed a hand on Bala's shoulder. "This won't happen again, hmm?"

"It's not a whole lot of fun when hungry mice race around in a person's empty stomach!" Bala said.

Amma clucked her tongue again. "The Festival of Lights is just around the corner, dear boy," she said. "You will come to our place for the special *Divali* sweets, *nai*?"

Bala's eyes lit up. "Will there be *laddu*?"

"I can promise that we will save the tastiest piece for you, and Basanta will let you have a *Divali* sparkler too."

Let him have one of my sparklers? I didn't want to share my *laddu* and I didn't want to give him a sparkler either!

But before I could protest, Amma untied the knot in her *pullo* and unpeeled two paper notes from a tightly folded wad. "Take this, dear boy," she said. "Buy yourself a meal."

She pulled me roughly by the arm. "Come!" she commanded.

Behind me, marbles rattled noisily, forcing me to look over my shoulder. Again Bala aimed his striker and *crack!* a shiny marble flew like a bullet. *"Arrey wah!"* he boasted.

I wanted to say something not particularly nice to him, but Amma told me to keep my eyes on the road.

I took a few steps, then glanced back. Bala was now trailing after a man, his voice suddenly whiny, one hand outstretched and the other rubbing his belly. "Sahib, one penny, if you please," he cried. "I have not eaten in two days!"

But the man in the suit yelled *"Hutt!"* at him and shooed him away like a fly from milk.

We left Bala where the road curved past the cobbler's shop and the bakery.

"Amma, why did you make promises about my sparklers before asking me first?" I demanded.

"Because everyone deserves a bit of happiness on *Divali*," she replied. "And what's wrong with a little kindness to a motherless boy, hmm?"

"Kindness for *him?*"

My mother tugged on her *pullo* and adjusted its drape over her head, ignoring my remark. "Take Gopal the Milk Man, for instance!" she went on. "He is kind and is rewarded for his generosity, don't you know! And his dear boy, Ganga, is just as honorable too! You give one and you get back sevenfold, that's what I say."

It was true. Gopal was a good and kind man. And his buffalo had multiplied sevenfold as news of his charity spread in the *busti*.

"Ganga's firecrackers were the loudest of all last *Divali*," I admitted. "They were so loud, Kalu hid behind the huts!"

"The point is," my mother inserted, "it's nice to be nice. *Bas!* That is enough. This conversation is not about fireworks."

But the conversation *was* about fireworks. Amma had told Bala that I would share *my* sparklers with him. Be nice to Bala? Why should I?

"It's not fair!" I stormed, but my mother's toe rings on the asphalt drowned my voice completely.

# Chapter 4

We had just passed the general goods store when Kalu loped around the corner. I bent down to stroke his head. *"Aiyyo!* Look, how his poor ribs poke out, Amma. I'll need an extra bone from the Big Kitchen to fatten him up."

Hollow of stomach and crooked of tail, Kalu roamed the streets by day but he usually settled down near my hut at sundown for the leftovers I brought from the Big House. Poor Kalu! Everyone chased him away with a *"Hoosh!"* and a *"Hutt!"* Who would be his friend, if not I? And where would he get his food, if not from me?

Kalu trailed along beside me with his nose to the ground, sniffing at blackened banana peels and crusty orange rinds. I gave his rump a friendly whack. "Stop following me, Silly Willy! I'll see you at the hut tonight, okay?"

Kalu stared up at me with adoring eyes.

"Go! Shoo!" I ordered, but he wagged his tail and stayed with me all the way to the Big Gate.

Amma and I got busy the minute we arrived at the Big House. She went straightaway to light the hearth fire with a matchstick. Her cheeks swelled like a wedding pipe player as she blew on the small flame, and before long, the kindling crackled, flames licked the soot-blackened earthen stoves, and smoke burst into the dusky room and stung our eyes.

I ducked into the henhouse to gather Little Bibi's breakfast eggs.

*Buk-buk-buk* squawked the hens as I groped around them in the dark. I found four eggs, smooth and warm, in the straw and nestled them in the fold of my *lengha*. I tried to be careful, but when I got ready to leave, one egg rolled out and fell to the ground with a splat.

I sucked in my breath. I was really in for it now! If Amma knew she'd mutter, "*Aiyyo,* Basanta! Why can't you be careful?" And if Little Bibi found out, she'd most certainly scream at me, "What? You not only steal, but you break eggs too?"

Quickly, I threw a fistful of straw over the broken egg and waddled out of the low henhouse.

"Missus Hen was lazy today," my mother said when I handed over the eggs.

"Throw in another onion and no one will know the difference," I suggested.

"Mmm-hmm." Amma sounded distracted. She moved about like lightning in the kitchen, now chopping, now stoking, now stirring. The bangles on her wrists tinkled as she worked, and the hissing fire made her forehead glisten.

"I'll sweep the rooms," I said, going for the willow broom, but my mother stopped me.

"Little Bibi's breakfast is ready. Take it to her now." She handed me the fully laden tray. "Don't dawdle."

"And if she questions me, what shall I say?" I asked.

"Hmm?" Amma draped a cloth over the food to keep the flies at bay.

"What will I say if Little Bibi asks about the ring?"

"Remember to mind the chickens along the way."

"Pay attention, Amma! What will I say to her if she asks about the ring, *hanh*?"

"Tell her you'll keep your eyes peeled for it!" Amma snapped. "What else is there to say?"

I turned to leave.

"Go carefully." For good measure, she added, "And do not trip."

"Okay, okay," I muttered. "Stop worrying so much."

No, I would make sure that I did not trip. There would be no more spills today!

I walked down into the Big Courtyard between the kitchen and the Big House, one stone step at a time, dodging hens the whole way. The tray was heavy, the food was hot, and Little Bibi was waiting.

The smell of egg and roti made my stomach rumble.

On some days, I got to have a bite from the leftovers, but I wasn't counting on such good luck today. Little Bibi would probably polish off her breakfast this morning and leave nothing for me.

Carefully, I climbed up the stone steps leading into the rear of the Big House. I had almost made it without stumbling or spilling anything, but my heart still thumped. Each step was taking me closer to her angry eyes.

"What will I say when she asks?" I wondered for the one hundredth time.

Little Bibi didn't say a word about the ring. She tilted her chair onto its back legs, crossed her arms, and waited to be served.

I set the tray down before her. "Did you find your ring, Little Bibi?" I asked.

There! It was out. A real thief wouldn't bring up the subject, would she? Might Little Bibi change her mind when she heard the concern in my voice?

But before my young mistress could reply, her mother said, "Don't talk when you are serving food!"

I bit my lip. I had forgotten about that rule. It was one of the many things I wasn't allowed to do in the Big House. I wasn't allowed to sit in a chair and I couldn't eat off a nice dinner plate nor sip from a crystal glass. I wasn't allowed to call Little Bibi's mother anything but *memsaab*, the polite address for a woman of her high station. I wasn't allowed to call Little Bibi by her real name, Munni, either.

I ducked back against the wall and waited for Little Bibi's reply. But my young mistress just pushed the omelet around on her plate, not even taking a bite.

"Your ring, Little Bibi?" I tried again from a safer distance.

"Enough about the ring!" she barked.

*Oo Maa!* Her words were like the thunderclap in the middle of the monsoon season.

"I only—"

"Fetch me a glass of water!" Memsaab commanded. "Go quickly!"

I scampered over to the étagère, where the earthen pitcher sat on the middle shelf. I tried to tip it gently by its long neck, but despite my efforts, water sloshed onto the floor.

"Careful! Careful!" admonished Memsaab.

While I was mopping up the spill with a rag, Little Bibi pushed away her unfinished plate and stomped out of the room.

"Clear the table," Memsaab instructed. Then, half to herself, she added, "I'll have to see about getting her a nice new ring for her birthday."

*A nice new ring.* That is exactly what she said. I heard her, plain as day.

After I cleared away the breakfast things I ran outside. I would find a rickshaw to take Little Bibi to school for a good price; then her frowns would surely change to smiles. "How clever you are to get a rickshaw for only two rupees!" she would say. And she might even add, "I'll teach you the *Angrezi* alphabet since you are so clever!" Yes, then she'd be sweeter than buttermilk. She'd be as lovely as a motia flower, like the ones blooming in her garden!

By now the road was bustling with the sights, sounds, and smells of a town up and ready for business. Bicycle and rickshaw bells sent pedestrians scurrying; the peanut man's singsong cry was sharp and clear: "Peanuts! Hot, hot peanuts!" The sugarcane press cranked out brown juice, the knife grinder's stone spun sparks, and urchins laughed and played. So many exciting things happened in a busy street.

But Little Bibi was waiting and there was no time to get distracted.

I stood at the Big Gate and peered down one end of the road and up the other, calling, "Rickshaw, rickshaw!"

As if he heard me, Ramu the rickshaw wallah pedaled around the corner, whistling a popular song from a movie. I flagged him down.

"Looking for a ride, little miss?" Ramu wiped his brow with his head cloth.

"Little Bibi needs a rickshaw ride to school and we're paying two rupees for the ride. Take it or leave it," I told him in my best grown-up voice.

"*Baap re!* You drive a hard bargain, little sister."

"And I suppose with the money you'll buy a black bead necklace for Rukmani, the chicken thief?" I teased.

*"Arrey baba,"* Ramu sighed. "Pity a poor man. Would you put in a good word for me with Rukmani?"

I gritted my teeth. Ramu was such a fool. Didn't he know that in addition to being a chicken thief, Rukmani was a brazen hussy? Didn't he realize that behind his back she winked at cross-eyed Ganga the Milk Boy precisely because he had a rich father? Lali and I had tried again and again to save Ramu from Rukmani, but he was utterly smitten. The poor man was a fool in love and there was nothing that we could do about it.

I left Ramu dusting off the seat of his rickshaw with his head cloth and ran back into the Big House. "Little Bibi," I panted. "Your rickshaw is here! For only two rupees!"

"You sure took your time!" said my young mistress. She didn't even thank me for my shrewd bargaining.

# Chapter 5

T he Big House was still and silent. Big Master was at his office and Memsaab was visiting friends in the elegant parts of town.

I grabbed the hand broom and went into the dining room. The shiny brown tabletop spread out before me; turbaned men in brocade tunics and pearls stared solemnly from gilded frames that hung on the wall.

I pulled a chair out, dusted the back of my *lengha*, and sank into the seat. How soft the damask was! I drummed my fingers on the table. "Fetch hot rice from the kitchen!" I cried. "Hurry! Hurry!"

I imagined that Little Bibi was my servant and I was ordering her around. "Hurry up!"

"Yes, Basanta."

"Shoo away the fly!"

"Right away, Basanta."

"*Tch*. Don't dip your fingertips in the glass!"

"Very sorry, Basanta."

"How many times must you be told? If you talk when you serve, you spit in the food!"

"A thousand pardons, Basanta!"

Little Bibi running to my beck and call! It was just too sweet. I stood, patted the seat to erase all telltale traces of my bottom, and rearranged the chair so that it was back to its exact place. Then I picked up the broom and got to work.

Though my strokes were steady, soft, and low, just the way Amma had shown me, the reeds still sent puffs of dust flying. *Swish...swish...swish.* I swept up rice kernels on the floor in the dining room, dust balls in the hallway, and bobby pins and movie magazines strewn in Memsaab's room. *Swish...swish...swish.* Through the Red Room and the Green Room I went, and next into the passageway, where the light was dim. The tall mahogany bookcase, filled with very old books with gold lettering, stood against the wall.

I straightened my back, now a little stiff from bending so much. *Oo Maa!* I was only half done! The clock in the hall struck ten and the sound reverberated through the house. I resumed sweeping, working my way from one end of the narrow hall to the other with deliberate and controlled strokes. *Swish...swish...swish...*and then...*ping!*

My ears perked up. I looked around for the source of the noise. It had come from under the big bookcase. I lay down and, cheek to floor, swept my palm along the floor from end to end. But I found only dust balls. I probed deeper with the broom and...*ping!* Aha!

My heart fluttered as I wrapped my fingers around the

object. Was it a coin that might buy me two tablespoons of sweet and sour *churan* wrapped up in newspaper? I pulled my hand out and opened it.

*Na!* It was not a coin at all!

Underneath the dust, the lost ring sparkled. Nine, ten, eleven stones and a tiny pit where the twelfth one once was. No matter—eleven stones were good too. I rubbed them against my *lengha* until the ring sparkled, just as it always had on Little Bibi's third finger.

I had found it: the very same ring Little Bibi had accused me of stealing yesterday! "Here it is!" I could tell her. "I found it where you dropped it, don't you know?"

But would Little Bibi then throw her arm around my neck and cry, "Sweet Basanta, you are invited to my next birthday?" Would she say, "How kind you are to fluff up my pillow and fetch my soft slippers"? *Na!*

I pressed my thumb against the stones. They glittered like the pomegranate seeds in Little Bibi's bowl.

Little Bibi was a rich girl. She had a pile of nice things. Nice clothes…nice bed…nice books…and soon, her mother had promised her a bigger and better ring.

I threaded my finger into the golden halo. It fit perfectly.

"Basanta!"

With shaky fingers, I took the ring off and slid it into my *choli.*

"Oh! Amma?"

"*Aiyyo!* Why so jumpy?"

"It's just…my back hurts from bending," I lied.

"*Tch,*" Amma clucked. "Rest it a while. I'll finish up in..."

I escaped from the room before my mother could finish, my heart beating like a drum. In the Big Kitchen, Tikki was imprisoned under my baby sister's arm. Durga was asleep; her rounded stomach rose and fell, and she didn't stir when I lifted her arm gingerly and retrieved my doll.

"There's a hole in her stomach," I had remarked when Little Bibi first gave Tikki to me.

"It's only a little one, silly!" she had replied. "And her eyes don't close properly. Otherwise, she's perfectly fine for you."

Yes, Tikki was perfectly fine for me—and a perfectly fine hiding place for the ring. I pushed my treasure into the hole in her middle, then hid my doll in the kindling pile, under a bunch of newspapers.

I sat in the shade of the henna bushes listening to crows screaming in the mango tree. The clock in the station tower rang four times. Little Bibi would soon return from school. She'd want me to put her school dress away and bring her biscuits to eat. But for now, I could have a little rest.

My heart was still racing in my chest and two voices were clamoring in my head. *Oi!* said one. *What have you done, hanh? Are you not now the thief Little Bibi said you were?* And the other voice said, *Oo ma! Little Bibi is a very rich girl and she's getting a better ring for her birthday and you will not be invited because you never are!* I held both my hands to my ears and repeated a song Little Bibi had taught me. She said it was a rhyme people from *Inglistan* sang to their children.

*JaknJil went updha hilltu*
*Fetchha pel of vaaater*
*Jak felldown an brokhis crownan*
*Jil com tumblin aaafter aaafter aaafter*

I sang it over and over again. I thought singing would calm my worried heart. But I was wrong.

# Chapter 6

The clock struck five and Amma and I opened the Big Gate to go home. It had been a long day, filled with curious happenings and jumbled-up feelings. I felt like I was in a dream inside a dream inside a dream

The walk home seemed unusually long. How many more steps until I could run to the tamarind tree? How much longer until I could be alone?

"Let's ride a rickshaw home, Amma," I pleaded.

"*Daiyya!* Why?"

*Because,* I thought, *I want to admire my ring and because I want to talk to Dinoo Kaka and to Old Nahni hiding behind a star and tell them that I wished really hard and my wish came true at last.*

I hugged Tikki to my chest and felt the weight of the secret that lay inside her. It reminded me of the fiery mango pickle and her countless cries of "Basanta, do this! Basanta, bring that!" Where were the smiles, *hanh*? Where were the "pleases" and the "thank-yous"?

"I'm tired of all this walking," I replied.

*"Daiyya!"* Amma exclaimed. "You've never complained before!"

A dip in the road made me stumble and I clutched my doll more tightly. I knew I had to hide the ring better as soon as Amma's back was turned, and I knew the perfect place to put it.

"Wash up," Amma told me as soon as we got home.

I ran to the water pump without being told twice. "I might be gone a while," I called over my shoulder. "I'll be visiting Dinoo Kaka too."

I threw some water over my face and sped to the knoll, looking out for Paki and Raju on the way. Luckily, they were not around. I sank to the ground under the tamarind tree, lifted up Tikki's dress, and fished out the secret hidden in her middle.

Now it was just me and the ring and Dinoo Kaka in the branches above, and he wouldn't breathe a word. I slipped the ring on my finger and gazed at it for the longest time. I held my hand out to admire it. As I twisted it this way and that, a ray of sunshine struck up a ruby red spark.

"Look, Dinoo," I cried. "Look how the ring shines against my skin!"

*"Caw, caw!"* Dinoo Kaka crowed in admiration.

*"Hanh,* Dinoo, it is very beautiful, is it not? But I have to put it away soon. Tikki's getting married in the next hour,

you see, and I must attend to a thousand things before Dear Boy's arrival."

As soon as my mother left to scour the pots with coconut husk and ash, I dived under Bapu's *charpai* and pulled out the Big Box. I rummaged under Amma's bright red sari and Bapu's white muslin kurta, teased up the splinter in the corner, and dropped the ring into the hidden little hollow, where it now nestled as snug as a bug in a rug. I pushed the box back under the cot, satisfied that my secret was safe for now.

When Amma had returned from the water pump, it took just a little cajoling to get her to agree to another wedding. Just as soon as the sweet milky tea and the *laddu* were secured, I ran to tell Lali about it. I warned her in no uncertain terms to be prompt and punctual.

As I waited for Lali to arrive with Dear Boy, I prepared for the wedding. I coaxed the pink back into Tikki's cheeks with the help of a little spit. I twisted her brown ringlets around my finger and creased the folds of her red bridal sari. I gently nudged aside the mica in my treasure box and picked out a tiny bead necklace for her to wear. My little bride was finally ready.

I looked about with satisfaction. The dowry was arranged for Lali's inspection, the tea was piping hot, and the *laddu* had been divided evenly into seven pieces.

But Lali and Dear Boy were late! I paced back and forth until Amma told me to stop skittering about like a cockroach, but it was hard to be still. My mind kept going back to the ring.

At last I heard a drumbeat, winding its way closer and growing louder by the minute. *Rat-tat-tat...rat-tat-tat!*

"They're coming! They're coming!"

"No need to shout," Amma admonished me.

I heard commotion outside. "They're here, Durga!"

Lali lifted the curtain and peered into our hut. "Ganga couldn't come," she announced. "He's helping his father mend the old cobbler's thatch. He's so sweet, *nai*?"

I didn't care if the Milk Boy was absent; that'd just mean more bites of *laddu* for the rest of us. But the crowd outside still seemed larger than expected. I turned to Lali. "Just how many wedding guests have you brought with you, *hanh*?"

"We are seven," she answered.

*Seven?* I counted by my finger joints: Lali, the mother-of-the-groom. Nandi, Pummi, Dev, and Hari, the groom's aunts and uncles. That did not add up to seven.

"Paki and Raju came too," Lali said.

"What? You brought Paki and Raju along?"

She rushed to explain. "They promised to be very, very good."

"And you believed them?" Lali was so gullible! Didn't she know Paki and Raju *always* spelled trouble?

But Lali quickly brushed me aside and assumed the

demeanor of a proper mother-of-the-groom. "*Bas! Bas!* Enough chitchat! Tell me about the dowry!" she commanded. "Is the bride bringing with her a large bed, a spacious *almarah* to hold her clothes, and plentiful kitchen utensils? What about necklaces, bangles, anklets, nose rings, and such? And did you include a pressed and starched dhoti and a fine wristwatch for the groom?"

"First you must come in." I stepped back to allow everyone to enter. "Welcome, welcome. Sit, sit."

Lali entered first, holding her head high. Dear Boy followed, perched upon Paki's shoulder. Behind him came Nandi and Pummi, singing a wedding song. Raju followed, beating a ghee tin can, and Dev and Hari brought up the rear, dancing the *bhangra* dance.

"Show the dowry, *nai?*" Lali demanded and I uncovered it for all to "ahh" and "ooh" over. I had scraped together a reasonable assortment of things: a few scraps of cloth, neatly folded; a small cushion for a bed; some old dishes; a matchbox chest; and a few other items.

Paki squinted at the pile. "What's that?"

"Those are brass pots for Tikki's kitchen," I explained.

"Is this a joke?" Raju asked.

"And that?" Paki pointed at a chipped teacup.

"It's a tub for the bride's bathwater."

"So nice," said Nandi, but the two boys clutched their bellies and laughed.

"Shut up, you *goonda* hooligans!" I shouted. "Mind your manners!"

"Ha. That thing's a *tub*?" Raju sneered at the chipped teacup. "Hee hee!"

"Get a load of the *almarah*!" Paki added, pointing to Bapu's shoebox. "Ho ho!"

"Beware!" I told him. "I'll run to your mother. Pentamma Mausi will twist your ears so hard you'll be sorry you came!"

"*Bah*! Good luck with that!" Paki said. "Amma's at the Big House, collecting a sack of laundry to wash at the river."

"What were you thinking, Lali?" I turned to my friend. The *goonda* boys were clearly ruining the wedding.

"Ho! What's this?" Paki had spotted the *laddu*.

I lunged and blocked his path. "*Oi!* Stay clear of the wedding feast!"

"The *badmaash* girl nearly knocked me over!" Paki shouted.

"I want a *laddu*!" cried Raju.

It got so noisy that Amma intervened. "So much *hulla goolla*! Take this ruckus outside," she ordered.

We gathered up the wedding things and ducked out of the hut.

"Here I come, carrying the splendid pots, tra la!" laughed Paki.

"Here I come with the lovely bathtub, tra la!" roared Raju.

"Stupid owls!" I muttered.

Outside the sun was blazing, but we went on with the ceremony.

When the time was exactly right for the bride and the groom to walk around the sacred fire seven times, Paki jumped up and snatched Dear Boy from Lali's arms.

"Let go of my son!" Lali protested.

"Will not!"

"It's my job to take him around!" she cried. "Give him back!"

"You can't do it! You can't walk properly on that lame foot!" Paki taunted.

Dear Boy was yanked back and forth, and before I knew what was what, the poor thing was on the ground in a little heap.

"What have you done, you donkey?" I screamed.

"Look! Look!" Lali shouted. One of Dear Boy's arms dangled from her hand, the other from Paki's.

"I knew it! I knew it!" I yelled. True to their reputation, the *goonda* boys had brought disaster yet again.

"You promised to be good!" Lali cried.

"A no-arm groom for a no-voice bride," Paki roared.

Lali and I ordered Paki and Raju to leave immediately, but they only laughed at us.

Amma poked her head out. *"Aiyyo!"* she scolded. "What's the trouble?"

At the sight of my mother, Paki and Raju turned tail and sped away like a bunch of cowards.

"Good riddance!" I shouted after them. "Amma! Look what they've done!"

Amma clucked her tongue at poor Dear Boy's condition. "Our handsome groom needs a bit of grooming," she said and took him back into the hut. A little later, she returned, biting off a thread with her teeth. "He's perfectly fine now, see?" She had patched Dear Boy up so that he could resume his marriage ceremony.

With Paki and Raju gone, the festivities continued late into the evening. We nibbled *laddu* and sipped milky tea to our heart's content.

At the end of the evening, we parted with vows to have another wedding before the year was out. I made Lali pinch her neck and make a god promise that from this day forward, she'd never fall for false assurances made by certain no-good, unreliable, and untrustworthy individuals.

# Chapter 7

The next day was Little Bibi's birthday party. I knew I would not be invited. I never was. My young mistress only invited her rich friends, who wore nice dresses and were driven around town by smartly dressed chauffeurs. But still, I hoped.

In the morning, between the sweeping and dusting, I made a jasmine garland just for her. After that, I worked alongside my mother to get everything ready for the party. Dishes and pans piled up in the kitchen as puffy turnovers fried to a deep brown, dumplings floated in creamy sauces, and the rice pudding was sprinkled with almond and pistachio.

In the afternoon, Memsaab sent me to the bakery for the cake. I knew the way like the back of my hand, because I had done it last year and the year before that, and also whenever Little Bibi had a random hankering for a sugar bun.

The birthday cake was so beautiful! It was decorated with flowers and creamy dribbles that crisscrossed like a garden lattice.

# Child of Spring

"What does the writing say?" I asked.

"Happy Birthday to Munni," the baker explained.

"That's her real name," I murmured. "And what is this?"

"That is the number 14."

I set down the rupees on the counter and the baker put the cake in a box. I carried it out into the busy road, Amma's warning ringing in my ear. "Walk, do you hear? Do not run!"

Amma worried about me constantly, but Old Nahni understood me so much better. "My sweet girl is a lusty bird of spring," she used to say. "And birds fly and they soar!" Dear Nahni, she had always understood me.

I was thinking about my dear grandmother when a cow ambled out from nowhere. Before I knew up from down, the clumsy cow had lumbered into me, knocking the box out of my hand. It fell, *smack*, onto the ground in the middle of the road! My jaw dropped and I sank to my knees.

"*Hutt, hutt!* Out of the way!" people shouted angrily. "Do you want to get killed, mad girl?"

With my heart in my mouth, I picked up the box and dodged through the traffic to the other side of the street. I squeezed my eyes shut and wished, *Please, please, let the cake be all right!*

I peeked inside the box. The pretty birthday cake was all topsy-turvy! Flowers drooped, leaves were tangled, and a crevice ran down one side! Devastated, I hurried back to the Big House.

47

Amma was suspicious. "Were you running?" she hissed.

"It was the cow!" I wailed. "I didn't see her coming! I didn't!"

With her lips pursed together, my mother went to work. She nudged flowers and repaired leaves and smoothed icing to camouflage, repair, and restore. But the poor cake was a bruised child, a wounded soldier, a bird with broken wing.

"Should I say the baker did a poor job? *Hanh?*" I ventured, but Amma clucked her tongue.

"Tell the truth," she said. "A lie will push you into the well, but a truth will pull you out."

"Maybe Memsaab won't notice," I said, mostly to myself.

Amma and I carried the cake through the Big Courtyard, up the stairs, through the back porch, and into the party room. It was already decorated with colorful crepe paper and balloons. The Big Table was laden with an assortment of treats, each one more mouthwatering than the other.

We set the cake down in the middle of the feast. I held my breath, stepped back, and gave it another long look. *It isn't too bad,* I thought. *Only a wee bit shaken up, that's all.* I wouldn't be unhappy to have such a cake for *my* birthday.

Amma and I placed the chairs around the table just so. I arranged the plates and the forks and knives and spoons just so.

When Memsaab entered the room, her eyes went

straight to the cake. My heart began to pound, *dhuk-dhuk*. I clung to Amma's sari.

My mother nudged me forward. "Tell all, Basanta," she said gently.

"It was the c-c-cow's fault, Memsaab," I stammered, but Memsaab didn't blame the cow at all.

"It was your job to be careful," she said sternly.

When Little Bibi came in, her glance skipped over all the other lovely party things and stopped at the bumpy cake. "What's this?" she asked, her eyes narrowing.

"Just a small accident in the road," Memsaab explained quickly, but Little Bibi was not easily appeased.

"What sort of accident?"

"The cow came too close, Little Bibi," I volunteered. "And the clumsy animal knocked—"

"Oh great!" she shouted. "What will my friends say to this ugly thing, *hanh*?"

Ugly? How could a cake be ugly? It was like saying your Nahni was ugly because she got a little old and a little wrinkled.

"I am sorry, Little Bibi," I said.

"A lot of good that does me!" my young mistress yelled.

Quickly, I handed her the flower garland I had made for her. "Felicitations!" I said. "Happy birthday, Little Bibi!" Then I turned to run back to the safety of the kitchen.

On my way out, I saw Little Bibi toss the garland aside. When it missed the chair and fell on the floor, she didn't even bother to pick it up.

Later, when the sounds of birthday songs and laughter sailed across the courtyard, I decided that things must be okay. The beautiful new ring from Memsaab had probably made up for the damaged cake—and for the missing ring that now lay in our Big Box under Amma's red sari and Bapu's muslin kurta.

# Chapter 8

I was so weary from helping out at the birthday party that I didn't really want to sit under the tamarind tree with Lali. But when I saw the white flower tucked behind my best friend's ear, I changed my mind.

"*Oo Maa!* A motia today! And who is the secret admirer?" I asked, fingering the petals. "Are you telling or not?"

"Go! Go!" Lali flicked my hand away in mock anger.

I bumped her shoulder with mine. It was time for a little fun. "Hmm," I said. "I am guessing the giver of this flower sits on tree branches to toss jamun berries at passersby."

Lali slapped my back. "Paki? *Tcha!* Are you mad?"

"Well then, let me see...the secret admirer likes to chuck marbles in drain holes?"

"Bah!" Lali cried. "If you are talking about Bala you can forget it. Really, Basanta! How can you say such silly things?"

I decided to ease up a little. "You can tell me, Lali. I'm your best friend."

Lali jiggled her foot and looked away.

"You may not want to tell me, but I know," I said. "The Milk Boy gave it, *nai?*"

"*Hanh!*" Lali tittered shyly behind her hand. "He came to the hut early yesterday."

"He likes you, Lali," I squealed. "A yellow flower and a white flower. This definitely proves it!"

I'd had a suspicion when I first caught Ganga looking at Lali, but I couldn't be sure. Now the flowers were proof, and Lali could no longer brush me off.

"What did the silly boy say?" I asked. "Was it something that sounded like this? 'O queen of my heart, c-c-come and ride on my b-b-buffalo's b-b-back.'"

"Go, go! It's not nice to make fun!" Lali cried sternly. "He can't help the way he talks."

"I'm just saying!" I giggled. "After all, the poor boy does stutter. And he's cross-eyed. When he looks at the rooster, you think he's staring at the crow!"

"He can't help that either, just like I can't help this." Lali thrust her bad foot out from under her skirt.

I hugged her as an apology and changed the subject. "I'm guessing we'll be planning a real wedding soon, *hanh?*" I asked, trying to coax a smile.

Lali poked me in the shoulder. "Go! Go!" she scolded in mock anger and then hid her face in her hands. "We'll have to wait until I am fifteen or sixteen, I think."

Lali and Ganga. Ganga and Lali. They went together

just fine—dear, sweet Lali and kind, gentle Ganga.

"What about Rukmani and Ramu?" Lali asked. "Do you think they will marry one day?"

I shrugged. Good old Ramu needed our help; we could surely find someone better than Rukmani, someone who was just as nice as he was. Lali and I talked about it, pairing him up with this one and that one, but nobody measured up.

"I am thinking Ramu and Basanta! Now that has a nice ring to it, *nai*?" Lali giggled.

"Don't be an idiot!" I scoffed. "His legs are spindly and he is much too old for me!"

Lali thought for a moment and then she snapped her fingers. "I've got it!" she cried. "Basanta and Bala! What do you say to that?"

"*Pshaw!*" I spat. "We're talking about Ramu, not me. Lali, now I know you are utterly and completely mad!"

Kalu trotted up to our hut promptly at sundown for his dinner bones. He crunched them for a while, then smacked his lips. He found his favorite resting place, circled three times, and sank to the ground, his nose on his paws.

I patted him on his head and tickled him behind his ears. He thumped his tail happily. "Hey, boy! Make sure you are alert tonight, hear?"

Kalu often joined us at night because he knew we'd give him a little something to eat. My parents were grateful for his presence. Amma said his bark was as good as a sturdy padlock on the door. Who would dare approach the hut with the dear dog standing guard?

The night was balmy and perfect for sleeping outdoors, so Bapu moved his *charpai* outside and Amma rolled out our sleeping mats on the ground next to him. The earth was hard under my back, but being able to look at the stars made up for the discomfort.

I searched for old Nahni in the night sky. She was up there, somewhere, Amma said, peeking from behind a star. Did my grandmother already know about the ring? Did she know her words had come to pass? Would she be happy for me, or would she moan *hai, hai* because I kept it instead of returning it to Little Bibi?

The day's events came back to me in a big rush. My young mistress had tossed aside the birthday garland, and no one had expressed one word of gratitude for the countless glasses of cold drinks I had fetched during the party. I sighed, turned on my side, and closed my eyes.

I fell asleep to the sound of the crickets and the toads talking to one another near the water pump. I slept soundly until bright and early the next morning, when I was awakened by the sound of Dinoo Kaka cawing.

I got up and headed toward the tamarind tree.

As I passed the water pump, Rukmani called, *"Oi, Basanta!"*

I slowed down.

"Off to carry on crazy conversations with the crow, *hanh*?"

I didn't want to be waylaid by that pesky girl. I had better things to do with my time than listen to her insults. Dinoo Kaka was hungry and I needed to get back to help Amma with breakfast.

"Some people might think that's a teensy bit loony, if you ask me!" she called after me.

"I don't know what you're babbling about!" I snapped. "Leave me alone!"

"On the other hand, some might think talking to crows is fine business. Do you, by chance, discuss the price of rice or the state of the nation with him?" Rukmani laughed.

"Shut up!" I broke into a run, my skirt flapping about my ankles.

"Leaving so soon?" Rukmani asked. "Come back and I'll show you something that'll make your eyes pop open wider than a gate. The stupid crow won't mind if you are a little late, I promise!"

I stopped. Rukmani was like a *Divali* firecracker—fiery and dangerous, but alluring and hard to ignore. "Okay. Show me."

"Not so fast." Rukmani spat out guava seeds with a loud *thoo*. "First you must agree to do something for me."

"What?"

"You must take this *laddu* to the Milk Boy."

"You're sending a *laddu* to the Milk Man's cross-eyed son? What about Ramu?"

I couldn't believe my ears! This...this chicken thief who stole chickens from her *memsaab's* coop and sold the eggs back to her! Why was she giving candy to Ganga?

"I don't care what the monkey-faced man Ramu says. It's my *laddu* and I can do what I want with it!"

"But—"

"But, *wut*, nothing!" Rukmani snarled. "Do you want to see what I have to show or not?"

Of course I wanted to see! Rukmani always had interesting things to show, especially the ones she pinched from her *memsaab*. And yes, I'd take the sweet sticky ball over to Ganga, even though Ramu's feelings might be hurt if he knew. And so would Lali's.

"Promise me first you'll go to the Milk Boy as fast as you can. Make a god promise and swear on your head!"

"Yes, yes," I said. "God promise and swear on my head and all that! Show me!"

Rukmani put the *laddu* in my palm, then pulled a rectangular slab wrapped in shiny paper out of her *choli*. "Look," she said proudly. "See this?"

"What is it?"

"Don't you know anything? It is a *chakalet*."

"*Chakalet?*"

"My *memsaab* eats it all the time. Do you want to see more?" Rukmani teased away the shiny paper, revealing a deep brown square. She nibbled on the edge and smacked her lips noisily. Her teeth and tongue were darker now.

"Is the *chakalet* good?" It smelled warm, sweet, and sticky. My mouth watered.

"Mmm-mmm. So tasty!"

The *chakalet* did appear to be very delicious.

Rukmani crimped the foil and tucked the *chakalet* back in her *choli*. "There's more."

More? What else had she stolen?

"And this is *leepshteek*, see? It makes your lips a pretty color." She twisted a glossy pink column up from a golden tube, then smeared it across her lips, turning them the same color.

Rukmani returned the tube to the secret part of her blouse with a smirk. She hadn't offered me a small bite of *chakalet* or a tiny smear of *leepshteek*. I couldn't believe I had been duped into a god promise that would make me a traitor to two dear people.

"You can keep those things, I don't care!" I growled. "What I have is one hundred times better!"

"You don't say! And just what would that be?"

"What I have is fit for a princess, that's what it is!" And then I realized I was making a big, big mistake. But it was already too late.

Rukmani's eyes widened. I could tell her interest was piqued. "Show it to me at once!" she demanded.

"I will not!" I was afraid of where this would lead.

"Liar! You've got nothing to show!"

"Maybe I do, or maybe I don't," I said, trying to climb

out of the big hole I had dug myself into. "Actually, there's nothing to show. I was only lying."

*"Aiyyo!"* she said petulantly. "Is it a bracelet or a ring? Tell me! Did your mother get it for your trousseau or what?"

"My mother and father are getting me lots of lovely things!" I said.

"Oh? And where does your mother put away those pretty things, hmm?"

"Wouldn't you just love to know!" I spun on my heel.

"Basanta!" Rukmani shouted. "You will take the *laddu* to the Milk Boy, or else!"

*"Hanh, hanh!"* I yelled back. "I will because I said I would, but not at this very minute, so stop pestering me!"

# Chapter 9

Amma spooned our dinner onto rimmed platters. We ate by lantern light, drawing rice and watery lentils into balls just big enough to make our cheeks bulge, and crunching onion and green chili for extra flavor. Inside the hut, the dying embers of the fire cast eerie shadows on the walls.

The sun descended behind the mango tree and twilight deepened. People emerged from darkened huts. One by one, cots creaked and mats filled. Everywhere voices hushed and movement slowed like a fan winding down.

Bapu carried his *charpai* outdoors and Amma pushed the Big Box into a darkened corner of our hut. With a snap of my wrist, I rolled out my sleeping mat near Bapu's cot and stretched out on it. The earth was hot under my back, even though Bapu had sprinkled water from a goatskin bag to try to cool it off. Just when the sky darkened, the little mutt Kalu joined us. A few feet away, Lali lay beside Vimla Mausi and the little ones. I opened my mouth to tell Lali about Rukmani and the *laddu*, but then I closed it quickly. Telling her could wait. She'd be too worked up to sleep if I told her now.

Farther away, Paki, Raju, and Pentamma Mausi lay still. The cobbler unwound his turban for the night and Ramu's *beedi* cigarette glowed like a firefly in the dark.

Everyone was out under the stars except Rukmani. Judging by the hazy light flickering in the cobbler's hut, she was finishing up her last chores, dousing the flames and sweeping the ash in her hearth.

I listened to the sounds of the night for a while. I turned over. "*Oi*, Lali," I whispered as loudly as I dared. "Are you awake?"

"Mmm...not quite." Lali's sleep-rimmed voice drifted over the prone figures between us.

"Rukmani's not on her sleeping mat yet."

"One never knows about that one."

"She stole *leepshteek* and a bit of *chakalet* from her *memsaab*, don't you know?"

"*Leepshteek*? *Chakalet*?"

"And the nosy thing wanted to know all my secrets!"

"What secrets?"

"Never mind!" I said and quickly changed the subject.

We counted stars until we came to the end of our numbers and then we searched for pictures in the sky. We found many good ones, but the best one was of Kalu.

"There's his paw and that's the tail. Do you see? Lali?"

"Yes, I see," Lali's words slurred sleepily. "Basanta, what is *leepshteek* and what is *chakalet*?"

"Oh! A *leepshteek* rises out of a little tube and makes a girl's lips pink and a *chakalet*..." I tried to explain about the *chakalet* the best I could. "Do you understand, Lali? Lali?"

But I got no reply. Lali was fast asleep.

Beside me, Amma wiggled into a better position and Durga lay sprawled and still. Bapu's breathing deepened. From farther away, the old cobbler's snores punctured the still night.

*Bhaun! Bhaun! Bhaun!* Sometime in the night Kalu barked and barked and woke me up.

Amma's mat was empty and so was Bapu's cot. Something was amiss. Though it was dark, I could glimpse a crowd milling around our hut, humming like a hive of wasps.

I jumped up from my mat and elbowed my way through the people, listening to broken bits of conversations: "*Daiyya!* Someone tried to steal into the hut!" "Anything stolen?" "*Aiyyo!*"

My heart skipped a beat as I pushed past concerned neighbors. "Amma?" I called.

My mother sat on her haunches, rummaging in the Big Box. The dim light of the lantern revealed lines on her forehead as deep as the ruts under the wheel of a bullock cart. All the best things she owned were stored in there—and along with them, unbeknownst to her, was the ring. I peered over her shoulder, my mouth as dry as dust.

"It's all here," she announced. Red sari, white muslin shirt, four bangles, two anklets, and the small pile of rupees saved for my trousseau.

I let out a breath. If those things hadn't been taken, it meant the ring was probably safe too.

My parents checked our hut for other things and found that they too were untouched. The bicycle stood in the corner and the umbrella hung safely from its nail. The tiffin box was also in its place.

Amma counted the stainless platters and the little *katori* bowls and all the brass pots. She checked the rice and flour levels in the earthen pot and she peered into the ghee tin. She even gauged the size of the kindling pile. The picture of the blue-black god still sat in its niche and the combs and bottle of hair oil were in their usual places.

"I'll look in the Big Box again," I volunteered, but my mother pushed me away.

"*Na.* No need of that." She ducked out the doorway, shoving me out ahead of her. Bapu nodded his head in answer to the silent, inquiring looks at the doorway: Yes, everything was fine. No, nothing was taken, thank the gods!

I heard a chuckle or two. After that, everyone shuffled back to bed.

I sank down beside Amma. "What time is it?" I asked.

"I heard the clock in the tower chime twice not so long ago," she said.

Amma's worst fears had almost come to pass. "How will a curtain keep a thief away?" she had always worried. Because there were no doors and locks for huts made from mud and straw, she had been extra secretive about our Big Box. "No outsider need poke a nose in it," she warned us with a finger to her lips.

But someone *had* tried to poke a nose in it, in the middle of the night, and if not for good old Kalu, the ring would surely have been stolen.

"Who do you think it was?" I asked.

"It's difficult to say." Bapu sank back onto his cot. "He was hidden under a shawl."

My head was abuzz. *Who could the thief be?* I ran down a list of possible suspects in my head. Paki and Raju had slept through the entire incident. Lali had slept deeply as well. The Milk Boy was too timid to sneak into someone's hut. And besides, his father was rich and there was no need for him to steal. Dear Ramu was too nice to do something so horrible. The peanut man was wily but he was not agile enough. Bala...well, he lived too far away to come to our *busti* in the middle of the night.

That left only one person unaccounted for: Rukmani! Yes, Rukmani was the number one suspect. Had she not wiggled and squirmed, prying for information about my ring? Had she not been missing from her sleeping mat? And wasn't she the only one *not* at the hut clucking her tongue and asking questions?

My mind was in such frenzy that I couldn't go back

to sleep. My palms were sweaty, my mouth dry. Had the thief taken the ring? It *had* to be there. It just had to! Why, I barely got to wear it! I hardly got to feel it on my finger. I hadn't had a chance to show it to Lali and watch her eyes grow to the size of *thali* plates.

I tossed and turned on my mat like a leaf on a windy night. New feelings and doubts tumbled about in my head. *If* I had put Little Bibi's ring back on her dressing table, as Amma would have expected me to, I'd be sleeping soundly under a starry sky instead of being sick with worry. *If* only I had not bragged to Rukmani. *If, if...*

I couldn't stand it anymore. I tried to get up without disturbing my mother but she stirred. "What are you doing?" she mumbled.

"I'll be back in a flash, Amma."

"Answer me! Where are you going in the middle of the night?"

"I'm only going to Kalu to pet him and tell him he's a good dog for scaring away the thief."

"Silly child." Amma rolled over. "Tell him I said thank you!"

I tiptoed past Kalu, who was breathing heavily. I groped my way into our hut and knelt by the Big Box, I slowly opened the lid, lifted the corner of the cloth, and eased up the little piece of wood. I probed the space underneath with my finger.

Nothing! The hollow was empty! The ring was gone!

# Chapter 10

I had lost the ring to a thief before my tongue could taste those sweet words—*my ring*. It was gone before my finger could savor its feeling.

I turned the Big Box on its side and searched in every nook by the weak lantern light.

Rukmani had to have taken the ring. Who else but her? She was a practiced thief and she'd itched to know about my secret!

I'd confront her at the first opportunity. "*Oi*, you chicken thief!" I'd scream in her face. "Give back my ring right now!"

The next morning as I started toward the water pump, I rehearsed the words in my head. "Hark!" I would say. "A chicken thief is now turned a ring thief!"

But then Little Bibi's voice rang sharply in my head. *Thief! Ring thief!*

And her eyes! I saw them too, plain as day. Just then Amma's voice flew out from the hut. "*Juldi, juldi!* We don't have all day!"

I picked up my pace. But when I reached the water pump, Rukmani was not there.

All day at the Big House, I felt as dreary as a snuffed-out candle in a darkened corner. I wandered from one room to the next flicking the broom at the floor, but my heart wasn't in it. The dull ache inside me just wouldn't go away. It just grew worse when I smoothed the sheets on Little Bibi's bed, and when I arranged her ribbons in a neat row on her table.

At last Amma clucked her tongue in irritation and sent me to sit in the shade of the guava tree. There, time came to a complete standstill. My mind kept running over last night's events again and again.

Rukmani! I was so angry I wanted to scream in her face here and now. But I was angrier at myself for landing squarely in this big mess. *Stupid, stupid Basanta!* I reproached myself, again and again.

It was the longest day of my life.

I went looking for Rukmani as soon as we got home, but her hut was as empty as a beggar's purse. I checked under the nearby mango tree, expecting to find her glossing her long hair with coconut oil. She was not there either.

To help pass the time while I waited for her return, I gathered some of the baby mangoes that were scattered about like plump beads. I thought I might eat some of the sour fruit or even play a game of jacks with them.

Rukmani's painted pots were stacked in a pile near her doorway. As wicked as she was, Rukmani was a great painter. When I ran a finger over the beautiful designs, the pile wobbled like the drunken cobbler at sundown. It would serve Rukmani right if her pots crashed to the ground and broke to smithereens.

But I moved away. It wouldn't do to mess with them. If I broke her precious clay pots, no amount of screaming about the ring would get me anywhere.

The clock in the station tower struck seven. If Rukmani didn't return within the next hour, I'd be back to square one and I'd get an earful from my mother as well for dilly-dallying. Gathering my courage, I lifted the curtain in the doorway to see if I might quickly poke around for the ring before Rukmani arrived.

"*Oi!*" Paki charged up like a bull stung on his behind by a bee! "Why are you snooping near Rukmani's hut?"

"I'm not snooping!" I cried.

"You were poking your nose in at the door like Ramu's goat! I saw you with these two eyes!"

"I...I came to—"

"You came to do mischief, I bet!"

"I came to admire the pots," I said as calmly as I could. "Why are *you* here?"

"To guard her house, of course. And it's a good thing I arrived when I did!" Paki shoved past me and began to circle the hut, making a great show of examining everything from thatched roof to floor.

"What do you think you're doing?" I demanded.

"I'm making sure everything is in shipshape order!"

"And why wouldn't it be, you crazy owl?"

"With suspicious creatures like you lurking about, who can tell what might happen?"

"Go away!"

"No way. I'm staying because something smells fishy!"

"Fishy?"

"Stinky fishy!" He circled the hut again and this time I ran behind him.

"Why do you care?" I yelled. "Rukmani doesn't give a hoot about you! Scat!"

"She needs me to guard her hut!"

"You only want her to bat eyes at you! She has no time for you. You're less than a fly on cow dung to her."

"Shut up!"

"It's the Milk Boy she's after. She's saved a *laddu* for him!"

"The Milk Boy?" Paki spun around. "What happened to Ramu?"

"*Hoosh!*" I threw a mango at him, and it bounced off his shoulder.

"*Oi!*" Paki hollered. "I'll get you for that, she-donkey! Tell me about the Milk Boy!"

I flung another mango and hit him squarely this time.

Paki dashed to the mango tree and came back running. His aim was true. *Phok, phok, phok!* He hit me on the shoulder, leg, head.

"Owl!" I dug into my stash and pelted him back. "Take that, and that!"

"She-donkey!"

Back and forth the mangos flew—*whiz! zoom! wham! bam!*—like frenzied parrots batting heads in a snug cage. A mango missed my head by a finger and bounced off the hut. Then another flew past my left shoulder and I heard a loud crack.

The pots teetered…tottered…and…*dhum!* They toppled over!

"Donkey!" I shouted. "Look what you've done!"

Paki's mouth was a big O. "It was *your* mango!"

"*Na!* Mine flew in the opposite direction!"

"It went straight for the pots!"

"Impossible!"

"Destroyer of pots!" screamed Paki.

"You're in for it!" I roared. "Rukmani's going to be madder than a striking cobra!"

"I'll tell her the whole story from A to Z! Your snooping started it all!"

"Pot breaker!" I yelled.

Paki looked around nervously. "We could tell her it was Ramu's goat," he said.

"It was no goat. It was a *donkey*," I insisted. "A donkey and a liar!"

We stared at the pile of broken pieces for a moment, then swept them into a heap with our feet and ran away.

Far into the night Rukmani ranted. I covered my ears till at last I heard the cobbler shush his daughter. *"Chup!"* he snapped. "Be silent! You will paint more pretty pots."

*It's true,* I thought. *Rukmani will make a new stack of pretty pots with her nimble fingers. If I had but kept mine behind my back in the Big House, I surely would not be chewing my fingernails down to the bone right now worrying and wondering what had happened to my ring.*

# Chapter 11

Another workday would soon begin. Bapu had pedaled off to the Public Gardens, Amma was washing at the water pump, and Durga was crawling about the hut like a confused cockroach.

"Come!" I commanded, but my little sister ignored me as she weaved in and out of the legs of Bapu's cot, colliding with the Big Box again and again and making circles on all fours like Kalu running after his tail. I snapped my fingers but it was no use. My little sister scooted further under the cot. "Disobedient girl," I muttered. "I'm going for Tikki and you better be out before I'm done!"

A gurgling sound made me turn around. Durga's arms and legs waved about in the air. Her happy coo had become a rasping croak.

"Quit that," I growled.

But my sister's arms continued to flail and the croaks seemed more desperate. Her eyes were wide as saucers; she sounded like Dev just before Vimla Mausi thumped his back to expel a tamarind seed.

*Oo Maa!* My sister was choking on a tamarind seed!

I snatched her from under the cot, turned her upside down, and whacked her on the back. She coughed a big rattling cough, heaved up a frothy blob, and began to cry.

I stroked her little back. Poor thing, how scared she was, with snot running out of her nose and tears pouring down her cheeks. But her breathing was more even now and her stomach had stopped heaving.

"There, there!" I soothed. "You've got to quit chasing tamarind seeds and peanuts! When will you learn?"

I scrunched my nose at the nasty mess at my feet, but then something caught my eye. I looked closer. *Arrey daiyya!* It was not a tamarind seed! It was not a peanut either. It was Little Bibi's ring! Durga had found the ring! But how?

I set my sister on the floor and pulled out the Big Box. On my knees I lifted the chip in the corner and eased a finger into the little compartment. I knew had examined it well that night. God promise, I had. But here the ring was and Durga had nearly choked on it!

I swept my finger from end to end of the space. *Arrey daiyya!* My fingertip felt the earthen floor of my hut. What was this? A hole? *Daiyya re daiyya!* Amma's frantic rummaging had caused the ring to fall through a hole in the secret compartment on the night the thief came!

"What are you doing in the Big Box?" My mother's question made me jump. I had not heard her return. "And is that not Little Bibi's ring?"

I blurted out Durga's story, hoping it might distract my mother. But after some cooing and clucking over my sister, she turned to me.

"Tell me about the ring!" she demanded.

I told her everything. Amma listened without interrupting. She let me have a little cry when I got to the part about the birthday garland that Little Bibi had discarded so cruelly.

When I was done, she said, "Now hear me, Basanta." And then she gave me the lecture.

Amma said she understood that I was upset because some people had so many nice things and some didn't. She also understood that it seemed unfair when some people worked hard to clean up other people's messes without being rewarded with fancy parties and birthday presents. But right was right and wrong was wrong, she said.

I lowered my eyes in shame even though her voice was neither loud nor angry. "Please, Amma," I begged. "Little Bibi's getting a brand new ring for her finger."

But there was finality in Amma's voice. "It's not yours to keep, Basanta," she said. "You must return it at once,"

"But what shall I say?" I asked.

"The truth. Tell her it was a mistake. Tell her it will not happen again. Beg for forgiveness!"

"You could say you found it today while you were dusting. Could you? Would you?"

The expression in my mother's eyes made me lower mine again. I didn't ask again.

I was so scared that I could scarcely walk straight. I'd gone over and over different lines in my head until I'd finally settled on the ones that sounded the best. "I found your ring when I was sweeping. I am so sorry I kept it, Little Bibi. I'll fetch you a glass of water, shall I? Shall I fluff up your pillow? Here are your soft slippers. What else shall I do for you today?"

Instead, when she turned around in her chair, I blurted out, "Little Bibi. I found your ring hidden in the China rug!"

As I handed it to her, I saw that she was wearing her new ring, much bigger and better than the old one. There was not a single stone missing from it. *Oo Maa!* How easily Little Bibi came by such nice things!

I was so flustered that I turned to run back to the Big Kitchen, but her voice stopped me at the door.

"Basanta!"

"Yes, Little Bibi?"

"You found it in the China rug?"

"Hidden in the flowers. You see, I never took it."

"What?"

"I mean, I found it for you. I didn't steal it."

Little Bibi shrugged, and then she said something completely surprising. "I never said you did."

I breathed in sharply. "But I thought...."

Little Bibi wasn't listening anymore. "I'm late for school." She stuffed her books in her schoolbag.

I started to leave, but Little Bibi caught me by the hand. "Basanta?"

"Shall I get you some water?" I asked, eager to get away.

She thrust the ring back into my palm. "You keep it," she said. "I don't want it anymore." She turned away and I knew I was being dismissed.

# Chapter 12

**M**ore than anything, I wanted to show Lali my ring, but there was something more pressing that I needed to do first. I found her up in the guava tree.

"Lali, I've got something to tell you," I called. "Promise you won't yell at me?"

Lali climbed down, one safe branch to the other. "*Accha*," she said. "Tell me."

And I told her the whole story about Rukmani and her strange request.

"You're taking *laddu* to the Milk Boy?" Lali shrieked.

"You promised you wouldn't yell," I cried.

"I'm only yelling because you made such a bad promise!"

I tried to reason with her. "I haven't done anything yet, Lali. I've waited till they were stale, see?"

"I don't care about that!" Lali cried. "I just can't believe you're going to do what she asked!"

"I have to," I explained. "If Rukmani found out I went back on my word she'd be hopping mad."

"What about Ramu? I thought he was also your friend!"

"But I've already given my word to take it to the cross-eyed boy, and a promise is a promise."

"Oh! Must you always say 'cross-eyed'? So rude, *nai?*" Lali stamped her good foot. "Anyway, it was wrong to make the promise in the first place! You know how Ramu feels about Rukmani!"

She was right, of course, and I didn't have a good explanation. "She tricked me," I said helplessly. "You know how wily she can be."

But Lali scowled and walked away in a huff. I didn't mind that so much. Being mad was much better than being sad, and I knew she wouldn't stay mad at me for very long. I ran after her and gave her braid a playful tug. "Will you go with me, Lali? *Hanh?*"

Lali swatted at my hand. *"Humph!* Go where?"

"To the riverbank?"

"You want *me* to go with you to deliver the *laddu* from Rukmani to Ganga? Are you mad?"

"Lali, if you go, you'll get to see him! And together we will give him an earful about Rukmani. Cross my heart."

I could see wheels turning in her head, so I gave her another wee push. "Please, Lali?" I begged.

*"Accha!* I'll go with you," Lali said finally, and then she added, "but I haven't fully forgiven you just yet."

We walked on, raising dust with our bare feet as we made our way through the field.

Along the way, I went over my predicament again and again. Then an idea popped into my head. *"Oi!"* I declared, stopping suddenly. "I cannot—I *will not* take the *laddu* to the Milk Boy. I will not be a traitor!"

"Neither to me *nor* to Ramu?" Lali asked, and I nodded. "God promise?"

"Yes, yes. God promise!" I said, and pinched my throat for good measure.

"What will you do?"

"Shhh," I hissed. "I am thinking." The riverbank was coming into view and I didn't have much time left to cook up a good scheme.

But after twenty more steps, my plan was in place.

"*Hanh.* I'm thinking I should tell Ganga something else," I said, giggling. "That would serve Rukmani right."

"Tell him what?" Lali asked in alarm. "Don't you dare without clearing it with me first!"

"Don't worry, Lali," I assured her. "I will tell the Milk Boy I have it on good authority that Rukmani sent him stale *laddu* because she thinks he deserves nothing but the worst and I will also say—"

"Wait!" Lali stopped me. "That would be telling a lie."

"Lali, Lali. Don't you see I'm on your side? I'm only telling little lies to make things better for you."

"Big or small, a lie is a lie!" Lali insisted. "And it's just not me who says so. Your mother—"

"*Hanh, hanh!*" I cut her off. "But don't you see? Sometimes when a person gets herself in a tricky place, she needs to bend a little rule here and there to protect...."

I was so busy laying out my defense that we didn't see

Ramu's goat or hear the tinkle of her bell. Suddenly, something nudged the small of my back, and before I knew it, I was on the ground!

"*Oo Ma!*" I cried.

"*Oo Ma!*" Lali cried.

The *laddu* fell out of my pocket and rolled in the dirt. Ramu's goat snapped it up before I could grab it.

"She's eating the *laddu!*" Lali yelled.

"*Oi!*" I raised my hand to swat at the goat, but stopped midair. Lady Providence, in the form of Ramu's goat, was disposing of the *laddu*, oh so neatly! "Good goat!" I shouted. "Eat! Eat it all!"

We clutched our bellies and laughed until we thought we'd die!

One part of me was saying, *Shame on you for not keeping a promise!* but the other was saying, *Lali's happy! Lali's happy!* It was a lot easier to listen to the second part.

"See, Lali? It was never meant to be!" I exclaimed. We watched the goat's hind parts recede as she ambled away.

"*Hutt, hutt!*" we heard Ganga cry. The riverbank lay before us. The Milk Boy stood waist deep in the water, his turban askew and his bare torso thin and wiry. His buffalo herd surrounded him, grunting and jostling and bellowing. He splashed water on their hindquarters, which were heavily caked with mud and dung, and prodded the noisy animals apart with a stick.

"Oh look, Lali," I said. "There's your man!" I cupped

my hand to my mouth and called out, "Ganga! *Oi*, Ganga!"

The Milk Boy looked up, his hand shading his eyes from the sun. "*Oi*, B-B-Basanta! What b-b-brings you here?"

"You'll never guess in a million years!" I shouted back.

"You came for a b-b-buffalo ride?"

"Not today, Ganga," I said.

"And who c-c-came with you?"

"Can't you tell?"

"The sun's in my eyes," he said.

"Liar!"

"You can tell him," Lali whispered.

"It's Lali!" I shouted.

"Lali?" And like a moth flying to the light, Ganga the Milk Boy came running.

After that, Lali and Ganga ignored me completely. I felt like a nasty weed in the middle of a bed of roses.

"Your first w-w-walk to the riverbank, *nai*?" Ganga asked Lali.

In her place I would have said right away, "Yes? So?" but Lali just lowered her eyes like a blushing bride.

"I have been w-w-waiting for this moment," he said.

"For what? *Hanh*?" I asked loudly but no one heard me.

Lali continued to be coy.

"W-w-will you have a ride on my b-b-buffalo, Lali?" Ganga asked.

"She will. She will! Say, '*hanh*', why don't you?" I prompted Lali, but she continued to stare at the ground and trace a big arc with her foot.

"*Hanh!*" she finally said.

"There!" I cried. "Let's go ride a buffalo!"

Ganga held Lali by the hand and led her down carefully to the riverbank. He left me to clamber over stones and rocks by myself. "Which one?" he asked her, pointing to his large and handsome herd.

Lali looked from one fine buffalo to the other.

"That one! That one!" I said.

But Ganga let Lali take her time. "I like that one!" she said at last.

And that one it was!

Ganga lifted Lali up by her small waist and perched her on the back of the buffalo. "Don't b-b-be afraid," he said. "I'll c-c-catch you if you fall."

"*Oi!* What about me?" I asked.

Ganga gave me a rough leg up on my buffalo. "Hurry up, *nai?*" he said.

Ganga rushed back to Lali, clutched her hand, and led her buffalo up and down the riverbank. When she wobbled on its slippery back or cried when it let out a bellow, he said with his eyes, *Fear not, dear one. I will always stay by your side!*

Me, he left to jostle about on my own.

Now was the perfect time to speak up. "*Oi,* Ganga!" I called. "Rukmani had a *laddu* for you, don't you know?"

The Milk Boy turned.

"She did? For me?"

"*Hanh.* But I don't think it was right! *Laddu* for you

should come from Lali and no other!"

"*Hanh,*" Lali said softly.

"W-w-worry not, dear Lali," Ganga said to her. "I w-w-would have thrown them to the b-b-buffalo, at once!"

"*Shabaash!* Well done! " I said and to Lali I added, "See Lali, Ganga loves you truly!"

"*Oo Maa!*" Lali giggled.

"What shall I tell Rukmani?" I asked as we headed for home.

"You can tell her the truth," Lali said, playing with the white flower Ganga had picked for her.

I nodded. I could say, "See Rukmani, I went to the Milk Boy and he said, '*Humph!* I'm throwing the *laddu* to the b-b-buffalo,'" which was not that far from the truth. Buffalo…goat; goat…buffalo. It was six of one and half a dozen of the other.

Ramu's goat sauntered toward us, her udders swinging, a yellow crumb still clinging to her beard. I had a feeling the *goonda* boys had something to do with her tether being untied. For once, I was thankful for their mischievous ways.

"What are you thinking?" Lali asked.

"I'm thinking that I should thank Lord Rama for Paki and Raju," I said.

# Chapter 13

It had now been three nights since Kalu had come to the hut. *Poof!* Just like that the little dog had disappeared—just like my ring.

"Kalu! *Oi*, Kalu!" I called for him all the way to the Big House, but he didn't come. "He's been gone for days, Amma."

"He's a dog of the streets, Basanta," she said. "He knows how to fend for himself."

When I spied the *goonda* boys in the jamun berry tree, I yelled, "*Oi!* Have you seen dear Kalu?"

"*Bah!* We already told you one hundred times we have no time to waste on a mangy dog!" Paki said.

And finally I asked Bala. "*Oi!* Where's Kalu, *hanh*?"

"Umm. Here, there, everywhere!" he said as he took careful aim and sent a marble flying into the air.

I was resting under the tamarind tree at the end of the day when Lali came up the knoll. "*Oi*, Lali!" I called. "Is there news of the dear dog?" But she had no good news for me.

Lali tucked her bad foot under her *lengha* and made herself comfortable next to me. "I have something nice to show you, though," she said, waving a feather. "I found it along the trail. So pretty, *nai*?"

"It's only a sparrow feather, Lali," I said. "People find nicer things all the time."

"Go! Go! What could be nicer than this?"

I showed her my ring. When Lali's face changed like the sky at sunrise, I knew it was far, far better than any bird feather.

"*Oo Ma!*" Lali gasped. "So pretty, truly! From your Bibi? She gives you very nice things, *nai*?"

"*Hanh*. From time to time."

"You are so lucky!"

"*Na*," I said. "*She* is the lucky one. Who is the one with servants to run and fetch for her all day, *hanh*?"

Lali examined the ring more closely. "*Aiyyo!* What's this?"

"It's only a little hole," I sighed. "One stone is missing. The others make you forget all about it. It's pretty enough for a nice wedding present when the Milk Boy takes you away in his bullock cart!"

Lali covered her mouth with her hand, but I could see that she was smiling.

"Did you get more flowers from Ganga?" I asked. It had been several days since the yellow flower had wilted behind her ear. "He should buy you green bangles for your wrist. His father is rich enough!"

"I don't need green bangles for my wrist," Lali replied.

"Don't be silly. Every girl worth her salt wants green bangles for her wrist."

"Not every girl," Lali whispered.

I looked at her. My friend seemed pensive today. "What's the matter with you? Why are you so mopey? Didn't your precious Ganga visit you in a sweet dream last night?"

"I tossed and turned all night," Lali replied.

"Because?"

"Because... Forget it. It's nothing."

"Because your precious boy came to pin another flower behind your ear in your sweet dream?" I prompted.

Lali shook her head and I tried again. "You tossed and turned all night because your precious boy *didn't* come to pin a flower behind your ear in your sweet dream?"

Lali stood up to go. "*Na.* There was no flower, and no Ganga, and no sweet dream," she said. "I tossed and turned because my mother let us eat from her plate and she went to bed hungry."

I stared at Lali again and this time I saw the worry lines.

"She tosses and turns at night," she said. "The rice pot is empty. There won't be much on my *thali* plate tonight, and there won't be any more sweet dreams for me at night either."

She said it so softly, I almost didn't hear.

"What will Vimla Mausi do?" I asked.

"She will not beg," Lali said.

"Perhaps her sahib will let her have some money from next month's wages?"

"She hopes his heart will soften when she goes to him," Lali said.

I tried to comfort her. "If his heart is like the Milk Man's heart and Lalla-ji's heart, it will soften."

Lali sighed. "I'm going home to be with her now," she said.

I wanted Lali to stay so I could put an arm around her neck and give her a hug, but she was already walking away from me.

I was really sad for Lali's family. Poor Vimla Mausi! Her luck had turned one year ago, when Lali's father fell from the scaffolding seven stories high. His cries rent the air for three days and three nights before they stopped, and Lali's mother was left with five mouths to feed on street-sweeper's wages. And now her rice pot was empty and payday was still two weeks away.

I was thankful for Amma and Bapu and for the food in our pots and for the sugar biscuits in square tins that Bapu brought home from time to time. The next time Amma cooked roti, I'd put mine aside for Lali. She needed it more than Dinoo Kaka, who could surely fend for himself for a day or two.

The smell of spice was in the air; my mouth watered

when I thought about the cashew nuts in the red butter sauce reheating on our stove. Tonight's meal was abundant because we'd carried home a lot of good leftovers from the Big House. There was some rice pudding too.

I thought of Lali, going to bed on a half-empty stomach. I thought about Bala too, and the mice probably running around in his stomach. Suddenly, I wasn't very hungry anymore.

The huts in my *busti* were silhouetted against the dark sky. Embers lay dying in soot-covered hearths, and last wisps of smoke escaped quietly through openings in walls. Pots clanged near the pump, where several women were collecting their water. The frogs kept up their nightly chatter and the crickets chirped loudly. An owl hooted in the neem tree.

I pinched my *lengha* between my knees and let the water fall on my feet. It was cool and refreshing.

The pail bumped and sloshed as I walked home, and my thoughts flew from the yellow flower tucked behind Lali's ear to the empty rice pot on her hearth.

After I unrolled my sleeping mat, I made a new mark on the hut to indicate yet another day since Kalu's disappearance. Amma had made me toss his bones away. I was getting very worried now that five days had passed.

Lali saw me making the mark. "Any luck?" she called.

"*Na*," I said. "It's time we organized a search party."

"*Hanh*. Pummi, Nandi, Dev, and Hari will help," Lali offered. "They're worried about the poor little dog too."

"That's nice," I said, stretching out on my mat.

Ramu rolled out his sleeping mat nearby and sank down with a groan. He was tired from pedaling his rickshaw all day under a hot sun.

"*Oi*, Ramu!" I called out. "Have you seen Kalu?"

"*Na*," he replied. "But I will keep my eyes open on my rickshaw routes."

I opened my mouth to tell him about Rukmani. I wanted to tell him that she was batting her eyes at the Milk Boy and plying him with gifts, but Amma was lying right beside me and I didn't dare. Instead I turned on my side and looked at my mother. Her breath was warm on my face. I stroked a tendril of her hair.

"Hmm?" Amma stirred.

"I was thinking we should do something nice for Vimla Mausi," I whispered.

"Yes. I heard about their troubles."

"Will you make some nice *dhal* and chappati to send?"

"*Hanh*, tomorrow, Basanta," Amma murmured.

I turned my face to Bapu's cot. "Bapu? *Oi*, Bapu?"

Amma jabbed a finger in my shoulder. "Shush!" she scolded. "It's enough you told me."

But Bapu had to be part of this too. "Bring home an extra tin of biscuits, okay?" I asked him.

Bapu did not reply. He was already fast asleep.

# Chapter 14

I served Little Bibi her breakfast, refilled her glass with water, and stood at attention with my back against the wall in case she wanted something else. Sure enough, her spoon clattered to the floor. "Get it, will you?" she said.

I dashed forward to pick it up.

"Mind that you wash it before you set it down," Mem-saab said, but she needn't have. I knew what to do.

I rinsed the spoon in the sink just outside the dining room and placed it close to Little Bibi's plate. Her new ring was hard to miss.

"Look, Bibi," I said, pointing to my own finger. "I wear mine everyday too."

"So?" Little Bibi said, chewing a mouthful of food.

*Oo Maa!* She didn't have to be so rude about it!

I buffed the ring against my cotton skirt. "I think it's beginning to lose its shine, Amma," I said.

"No time to talk about the ring just now." Amma's eyes were on the embers in our hearth.

"It's really looking quite old, see?" I held up the ring but Amma focused on her dinner preparations. "I mean, it's not even half as good as Little Bibi's new ring, is it?"

"*Chi*, Basanta!" snapped Amma. "Why do you babble so? It was good enough not so long ago. What has changed between then and now?"

*It's Little Bibi's new ring*, I said to myself. *Her new ring is making me change my mind about this old one.*

My mother dished out a portion of food in a stainless steel box and tied it in a square cloth. "Take this to Lali's family," she told me.

I walked fast to keep the food warm. "Mausi! Look!" I called when I was ten paces from her door. As soon as the sharp, tangy aroma of *dhal* wafted in the hut, the little ones came scurrying.

"Basanta, daughter!" Vimla Mausi cried and her hand stopped at her mouth.

Lali wrapped her arms about me. "I just knew in my heart," she whispered in my ear and we looked and we saw ourselves in each other's eyes.

Vimla Mausi measured out portions carefully. I saw that hers was the smallest of all.

Their predicament gnawed in my head like a mouse nibbling on grain. I was grateful for Amma but there had to be another way to keep Mausi's rice pot filled.

On the way back home, I stopped beneath the tamarind tree to visit with Dinoo Kaka. "Look, Dinoo," I cried, waving my hand in the air, "My ring is beginning to be as tired and faded as Tikki. Don't you agree?"

The feathery tamarind leaves swished with the breeze. *Caw, caw,* Dinoo answered from above.

"*Hanh,*" I called back. "You are right, of course. A ring is a ring, even with a red stone missing and a band less golden. Tikki? She's well, thank you. She may be ragged and old, but she makes my heart very happy."

I leaned against the broad trunk and my mind hopped from place to place—from the Big Kitchen to the jamun berry tree to the riverbank—and then it rested on Lali. *Poor Lali,* I said to myself. *She has less in her cooking pot than I have on my finger.*

Dinoo cawed again. I think he too had Lali on his mind.

Then, from not so far away, I saw Paki and Raju's heads bobbing my way.

"*Oi!*" I yelled. "Turn back right now!"

"We're coming for tamarind and you can't stop us!" Paki said.

"You won't find any. I already looked!"

"*Bah!* Big Brother, I'm betting the sty in her eye would keep her from finding her own rear end if she went hunting for it!" Raju scoffed.

"Don't come up here!" I warned.

"You don't own the tree," Paki growled. The *goonda*

boys circled the tree twice.

"Owls! I've told you already you won't find any tamarind!" I shouted.

"You're always under the tree, stealing tamarind for your mother's pot," Paki said.

"Lies!" Didn't they ever quit? Wasn't it enough that they had ruined Tikki's wedding and broken Rukmani's pots?

"I bet they're under her bum!"

"Oh ho!"

Two pairs of eyes glinted wickedly.

"On your feet!" Raju barked.

"There's nothing under me!" I said. "Go away!" I held my hands up to ward them off.

Paki's eyes narrowed. "What's that thing on your finger?"

"It's not a tamarind," I said.

"Hand it over!"

They tried to pry the ring off my finger and I fought back. But Paki put me in a headlock and Raju was rolling up his sleeve menacingly.

"Get it, brother!" Paki yelled and I squeezed my eyes shut. I couldn't fight them both off and there was no way out either. Helplessly, I waited for the ring to be forced from my finger.

But luck was on my side.

Pentamma Mausi strode up just in the nick of time. "*Oi!* Didn't you hear me calling and calling?" She twisted their ears so hard it made them squeal.

"Ow! Ow!"

"Let go, Amma!"

"You untied Ramu's goat again!"

"*Na*. Lies, all lies!" they protested.

Paki and Raju hollered but it was no use. Their mother dragged them both away, wriggling and squirming and yelling.

With the *goonda* boys gone, I settled back under the tree to resume my thoughts about Lali. There was an idea and a plan forming. *Yes*—I talked myself through the plan—*you must do this first and next, you must do that.*

I pushed up, dusted off my palms, and headed to the grain store.

# Chapter 15

I heard Lalla-ji's booming voice even before I saw him. The grain merchant sat cross-legged on the white cotton floor-spread, barking orders to his men: *"Oi!* Put the rice in this corner! The wheat goes there! The barley next to the millet!" In response, they grunted and scurried about like ants.

He held a scale that teetered and tottered as he added or took away each iron weight. Behind him, a dozen bins filled with lentil and grain were lined up like docile children. The goddess of wealth, bathed in flowers and incense, smiled from her pedestal.

I greeted him, my palms joined together. *"Ram Ram,* Lalla-ji."

*"Ram Ram,"* he called back. "What brings you here at this hour?" His eyes twinkled behind spectacles that were halfway down his nose. His belly spilled over his lap under a see-through muslin shirt.

"We are running low on rice, you see."

*"Hanh."* Lalla-ji nodded sympathetically. "It's near the end of the month, after all."

People's supplies of rice, lentils, and flour often ran out this late in the month, and they lined up at his shop with cloth bags, eager to fill their pots again.

The grain merchant set the dipper down. "Is everyone well at home?"

"They are well, Lalla-ji."

"Did your mother send you for the rice?"

"She doesn't know that I am here," I said quickly.

"Oh?"

"I want to surprise her, you see."

The merchant chuckled. "I will measure out as much as you can carry back safely," he said. "Did you bring money with you?"

"No. But I have something better." I held out the ring.

Lalla-ji peered over the rim of his spectacles. "What's this, my girl?"

"You can keep it," I said. "It will pay for the rice."

It was the only thing of value I had to bargain with, the only thing that would make Lali's dreams sweet again.

The merchant turned the ring over in his hand. "Hmm. Where did you get this?"

"It's mine, Lalla-ji," I answered. "Honest."

Lalla-ji scratched his bald pate. "I don't know..."

I didn't know why Lalla-ji sounded so unsure. Did he think the ring was a fake? Or perhaps he was worried that I had stolen it?

"It's a very nice present from my Little Bibi," I said, "and you won't be sorry to have it, I promise."

The merchant swatted at a fly and sent it humming.

"Please, Lalla-ji?"

The grain merchant mopped his neck and brow with the cloth. "*Uff oh!*" he groaned. "Today this heat will surely kill me!"

A rickety fan turned weakly, like an old lady looking this way and that. The breeze made Lalla-ji's muslin shirt billow out. *Tick, tick, tick.* I waited for his decision.

"*Accha,*" he said at last. Grunting, Lalla-ji scooped rice from his sack with a measuring tin and poured it into a bag. He placed the bag on the scale. "Two *ser,*" he said. "Carry it carefully."

I was so happy I wanted to shout. Two *ser* of rice would carry Vimla Mausi through until her wages flowed again. I held the bag in the crook of my arm and turned to go.

"*Oi.* You forgot something!" Lalla-ji held out the ring.

Why was he giving it back to me? "We made a fair trade," I told him. "The ring is yours to keep."

He smiled. "A pretty ring for a pretty finger."

"But it's a nice ring. Lalla-ji. You could sell it for a lot of rupees."

"Keep it." He swatted at the fly again and missed. "Tell your good parents I send them my greetings and wish for their troubles to be over soon."

"I will," I said, and added quickly, "But you must not talk about the ring. Make a god promise and swear it on your head."

The merchant nodded. *"Accha-ji.* A secret is a secret," he chuckled and his big stomach jiggled.

I took the rice to Lali's hut. I hoped to see Vimla Mausi's eyes light up like the stars. Instead, I saw great sadness in them.

"First you bring me food from your pot and now you bring me this," she sobbed.

*"Aiyyo!"* I cried. "The food wasn't tasty? My mother is a very good cook!"

With a cry, Vimla Mausi pulled me close. *"Na,* dear Basanta," she whispered. "I am grateful for the generosity. Your dear mother has a heart of gold!"

I opened my mouth to tell her the whole story, but I didn't want to brag. Amma always said the left hand must not know what the right hand gives, so I kept my mouth shut.

"It's not so much. The rice will probably last only for a few days," I said.

"In one week I will collect my wages," Vimla Mausi said with a smile. "And I will repay your mother."

"Mausi!" I cried. "Amma is happy to help."

And I was happy that the rice pot would bubble in Lali's home that night. Perhaps she would have sweet dreams about the Milk Boy once again.

# Chapter 16

On Saturday, Lali came to my door. "Come, quickly!" she urged. "The fight's ready to begin! Do you hear the shouts?"

A big fistfight always preceded the Great Battle of Kites. It always lasted exactly twenty minutes. Words were flung in the first half, and fists in the second.

And each year, the question was the same. Who was going to be the number one champion kite flyer of the *busti*?

I wondered who would be victorious this time.

Paki would say, *Who else but I?*

Bala would say, *In your dreams!*

Then words would turn to blows and everyone would egg them on from the sidelines, clapping and cheering.

I hiked up my skirt to go join Lali, but Amma stopped me.

"Please, Amma," I begged. "I'll be back just as soon as there is a knockout!"

"Let her go," Bapu said. "It's harmless enough."

My mother shook her head and went back to stoking the fire.

I threw my father a grateful look and ducked out of our hut. "Did it turn into a fistfight yet?" I asked Lali.

"It...it may be too early for that," she panted.

"Do you think Paki will win?" I asked.

"Hard to say," Lali replied. "He says he'll vanquish fifty kites before the season is over. We must hurry. Things will be starting up any minute!"

Up ahead we saw the washerwoman kicking up dust, her sari hitched high and a twig in her hand.

"Uh-oh! Paki's mother's got wind of the fight!" I cried. "We've got to get there before she ruins everything!"

But by the time we reached the field, the washerwoman was already pushing through the gathered crowd.

"It's no use," Lali sighed. "We're too late."

She was right.

"The fight's over," Nandi announced when she saw us approaching.

"Who won?" I asked.

"Bala threw some good punches," Pummi replied. "But Pentamma Mausi came and sent him scurrying."

"Big Brother had victory just about wrapped up in his back pocket, so I'd say he was the winner," Raju boasted.

"No, no. It was the other way around," Hari said. "*Dhushoom! Dhushoom!* Quick jabs to the chin and shoulder and Paki was flat on his back!"

I turned to Lali. "Thanks a lot!" I snorted.

Lali held up her hand. "What?"

"You should have come for me a lot sooner, that's what!"

I ran to catch up with Paki, now dodging his mother's stick.

"Hey!" I called to him. "I heard you got beat good and plenty!"

"Get lost!" he shouted.

I ran up to Bala next. "Say! I heard you got thrashed good and plenty!"

"Beat it!" he growled.

When it was nearly time for the kite battle, Lali, Nandi, Pummi, Dev, Hari, and I formed a tight circle near the rim of the field. We each readied our stash of tamarind seeds to place our bets.

"Bala, 6 to 1!" I declared. If he won, I'd make a tidy profit of six tamarind seeds for each one I wagered. I tossed twenty seeds in the center of the circle.

"Are you sure?" Lali asked. "Did you forget he lost to Paki last year?"

"He's going to win," I said with a burst of confidence. "You should back him too."

"Bala, 3 to 1!" Lali cautiously added her modest share of ten to the seed pile.

Nandi followed suit, but she only had six seeds.

Twenty plus ten plus six. That was not even remotely close to the one hundred and twenty I had counted on winning. Pummi, Dev, and Hari had enough seeds in their bulging pockets to ensure me my win, though. They were whispering fiercely amongst themselves and I could tell they too were favoring Bala. So I did some fast talking. Soon I had the silly things nodding in agreement, and now I was one step closer to a big win.

"Paki, 20 to 1!" they declared. They emptied out their pockets, making our collective pool very large!

"*Shabaash!* Bravo!" I cried. "I'll guard these because I am the bookie." I swept up the last of the tamarind seeds—all one hundred and fifty of them.

The two rivals entered the field to loud cheers and catcalls. Bala and Paki were each armed with five brilliantly colored kites and large spools bulging with line. They also carried smaller spools of *manja* thread, the dangerous fighter string coated with powdered glass. *Manja* was as sharp as a razor, and the winner would use it to slice the opponent's kite away from its line.

Like warriors in a fighting ring, both boys strutted like roosters. Each made a show of tying the *manja* to the harness of his kite and then securely attaching the longer line.

If Amma were here, she'd cluck her tongue. She didn't understand kites. "*Tcha!* That Bala!" she would mutter. "Never enough money for food but always plenty for his precious kites!"

Bala waved to the crowd and took his bows like a champion kite master. I was rooting for him all the way. There was a big pile of tamarind seeds at stake!

He was at a disadvantage because of his defeat last year, but I didn't care. I was 100 percent certain that Paki had cheated in that contest. The kites had been locked in a deathly embrace. Bala had backed up the length of the field. Raju had slyly stuck out his leg, and Bala had gone down. That's how Paki had won.

I was determined to make up for that this year.

I ran to Paki's corner. "Do you have a strategy in place?" I asked.

Paki was securing the *manja* thread to the harness of Jhansi-ki-Rani, a garish pink kite. Paki named his kites after important and heroic persons. The greater the importance of the person, the greater the power of the kite—or so he claimed. He was saving Maharani, his finest kite, for the decisive final round.

*"Hoosh!"* He waved me away. "Only a fool would divulge secrets to a spy from the enemy camp!"

I moved in closer, faking an interest in Jhansi-ki-Rani, but Paki shuffled sideways like a crab. "Stay away from my kite!" he growled.

"Are you sure she's a match for Shivaji-the-Mighty? Bala's sending up Shivaji first, you know. It's a brilliant strategy, if you ask me."

"A fat lot you know about kites!" he said. "Get out!"

Paki was good and riled up now, just the way I wanted him. If he lost his focus, he'd be more likely to lose the battle and I'd win a huge pile of tamarind seeds.

"I hear the Milk Man is planning a celebration party,"
I went on. "And guess who the guest of honor will be? Not
you, I'll bet!"

My taunts made Paki so mad that he spun around on
his heel to lunge at me. Before we knew what was what, his
fingernail had gouged an ugly tear right down the middle
of the pretty Jhansi-ki-Rani.

"Oops!" I said. "Now look what you did!"

Paki's jaw dropped. "Oops? Look...look what *I* did?" he
sputtered. "It was all your fault!"

"Yeah, you horrible, *badmaash* girl!" Raju added.

"I was just making conversation." I backed away
quickly.

"I paid good money for this kite, and you ruined it!"
Paki yelled.

"It was your fingernail!" I said.

"You're a spy and a destroyer of kites!" Paki shouted.

"Your dirty fingernails are longer than the dirty nails on
a sadhu," I said. "Why don't you do something about that?"

"Why don't you pack yourself up in a jute bag and go
far, far away and never come back!" Raju roared.

"*Oi!* What's the ruckus?" Bala called from the other end
of the field. "Are you ready for battle or not?"

"Change of plan!" Raju announced. "Change of plan!
We are using Akbar-the-Great!" He held up a majestic new
kite, as green as a glossy guava.

"No fair! What happened to Jhansi-ki-Rani?" Bala
asked.

"It's Akbar-the-Great, okay?" Paki yelled back. "Take it or leave it!"

"Bring him on!" Bala shouted. "Akbar-the-Great, Jhansi-ki-Rani—it's all the same to me!"

I ran to join Lali waiting on the sideline. She moved over to make room for me. "What was all that about?" she asked.

"Oh, just a teeny mishap," I replied. "I wouldn't worry too much if I were you."

I crossed my fingers and waited. Paki was still hopping mad, and that meant wouldn't be at his best during the contest. I was counting on that.

The battle of kites lasted the better part of the morning. Akbar-the-Great went up against Shivaji-the-Mighty, fierce black against brilliant green. They made a fantastic spectacle in the sky, whirling, swirling, dipping, and soaring. Paki and Bala tugged, gave slack, and maneuvered their kites into spins and loops to wild roars from the crowd.

Paki's Akbar-the-Great emerged victorious at the end of the first battle, but Bala didn't appear worried. Cool as a cucumber on a hot day, he pulled out the kite he called General.

I watched entranced, biting on my fingernails, every part of me quivering.

And so it went. Akbar-the-Great versus General; General versus Dilip Kumar; General versus Mahatama Gandhi. On and on the war raged, battle after battle, to jubilant cries of *Bo Kata!* from the victors.

*"Wah! Wah!"* shouted the spectators, each time a vanquished kite drifted sadly away, tail fluttering and severed line trailing.

Two hours later, the score was dead even. Bala's Lodhi had just defeated Mahatama Gandhi. Paki had brought out the fierce Maharani for the final round. Bala would fly Lodhi again. This was the moment everyone was waiting for.

"Get him, Bala!" I screamed.

*Paki! Paki! Bala! Bala!* The crowd was going wild.

The combatants rolled up their sleeves and prepared for the decisive thrust. And when the wind was just right, Paki and Bala nodded. Raju and Dev got the kites into position and let go. Maharani and Lodhi rose majestically and fearlessly skyward.

I held my breath.

Up the kites climbed, goaded by the rush of wind. Soon they were mere specks, ready for the strike. Lodhi and Maharani dove at each other like fighting cocks, circling, sometimes teasing, sometimes enraged. They jabbed and pecked at one another, now wild and erratic, now determined and purposeful. The kites would fly close enough for an embrace, then dart away and hover at a distance from one another, tense and watchful.

At last it was time for the kill. Who would deliver the fatal blow? Sweeping their arms wide, Paki and Bala sent their kites into the final death embrace.

I sucked in my breath. "Do it now, Bala!" I screamed. "Slice! Kill! Pulverize!"

Bala and Paki each galloped backwards across half the length of the field, heel over toe, raising clouds of dust under their bare feet. Hand over arm, they reeled in the string.

Beside me, Lali sucked in her breath. "Who will it be?" she whispered.

Our eyes were glued to the sky. Who indeed?

And then it happened. Maharani broke away from her tether and wobbled away on a wind current. Lodhi was victorious! Bala had won!

"*Bo Kata!*" Bala's final victory cry rent the air. He grinned from ear to ear.

The crowd lifted him onto their shoulders and cheered: "Long live Bala! Long live Bala!"

Then I caught sight of Paki coming toward me, a threatening scowl on his face. He charged like a mad bull and kicked dust at me. "It's your fault!" he screamed.

"Don't be silly!" I retorted. "Jhansi-ki-Rani was not even your trump card. How can you blame me?"

But I didn't push my luck. I walked away quickly because when Paki got like that, there was no telling what he might do. I ran to get the seeds and joined Lali, Nandi, Pummi, Dev, and Hari to settle our account.

I had won big! Poor Pummi, Hari, and Dev... Well, I did feel a little sorry for them!

# Chapter 17

Amma stoked the fire in the Big Kitchen, then kneaded the dough until it was soft and pliable. I helped chop up the onion and the fresh coriander for the egg curry. Little Bibi was waiting for her breakfast.

"No money for food, but plenty to spend on kites!" Amma grumbled.

"Bala collected a pile of coins at the end of the match," I told her.

"How so?" Amma's fingers were now coaxing Little Bibi's roti to puff up like a golden balloon on the smoking griddle.

"He got other people to wager real money just like a bookie. He talked a good talk so the people who won didn't win a lot and the people who lost, lost big—enough to give him some to keep for himself. Pretty smart, *nai*?"

"*Tcha!*" spat Amma.

"My pocket would be bulging with coins too if I had wagered real money," I said.

"*Nonsense!*" she snapped. "Careful what you say, little miss!"

I quickly brought the subject back to Bala. "He's going to be making some good investments with his money."

"Such as?"

"He didn't say exactly."

"That Bala," Amma mumbled as she stirred the pot. "He's nobody's fool."

Rukmani's chickens squawked and flapped as Dev sprayed water at them, trying to drive them away from the water pump. Little Hari was getting a thorough soaking too. His hair was plastered to his head and his shirt was stuck to his back. Dev bent over laughing at the chickens as they ran about crazily.

"It's not one bit funny!" I yelled. "Vimla Mausi's going to be madder than a hornet if Hari catches a cold!"

"Lali says it's okay to have a little fun," Dev whined. "She's our big sister and she can tell us what to do but you are not allowed. You're not our boss. So there!"

I wanted to walk over and smack the impudent little thing right then and there, but I had more important things to attend to. "Where is Lali?" I barked.

"Go find her yourself!" Dev said.

I couldn't believe it! I stomped over to their hut and found Lali picking out little stones from the rice. "Did you hear the mouth on that child?" I asked.

Lali looked up from her winnowing basket. "Who? What child?"

"Your brother Dev, that's who. He's getting too big for his britches. I can't believe you let him talk back like that! If Durga was ever that cheeky, why, I'd pin her to the wall by her ears."

"Durga knows only how to coo."

"Lali! That is *not* the point!"

"Basanta, Basanta. Tell me what you're upset about, *nai*?"

I told her everything, starting with Dev's backtalk and ending with Hari being soaked to the bone.

"Hari's wet?" Lali jumped up. "*Oo Maa*! I didn't know!"

"You can't know about everything, Lali," I soothed. "But you should know about Dev and you should do something about him."

"He learns from others." Lali rushed off to the water pump. "He follows Paki around like a puppy, lapping up everything that falls from the rascal's mouth."

Lali went to find Dev and Hari and I went looking for Bala. I found him at the far rim of the field, chucking jamun berries at passing motorcars in the road. "*Oi*. Have you seen Kalu?" I demanded.

"Don't you ever give up?" Bala asked.

"Come, come. Spit it out!"

"He's in *Inglistan*, shaking a paw with the great rani."

"Rubbish!" I snapped. "Owl!"

"You are the number one owl to carry on and on about that scrawny mongrel."

"You better tell," I said. "The poor thing's probably ready to die from hunger at this very moment and nobody else cares about him!"

*"Arrey baba,* enough of your high drama!" Bala smacked his forehead with his hand. "I bet your darling puppy is hale and hearty and being looked after like a prince."

"Impossible! Poor Kalu's got nowhere else to go. No one loves him like I do!"

"I wouldn't bet on it." Bala turned away and threw another berry. It struck the side of a car with a *thwack.* And that's when I figured out that he knew. It was written all over his face.

"Tell me!" I demanded.

"I don't have to tell you anything!" Bala said. "I am a master kite fighter and you can't make me!" He spun on his heel and ran away.

I watched him dash to the other side of the road, where he mingled with the pedestrians, holding out his hand. In less than a minute, he had switched from master kite fighter to master beggar.

I replayed the confrontation with Bala in my head, step by step, frontward and backward. All my shouting and yelling had gotten me nowhere. I should have stayed calm and cool. I should have reminded Bala about the promised *Divali laddu.* That would have been the smarter thing to do.

I retraced my steps home. There was a boisterous game of *Kabaddi* underway on one side of the field. A boy sent in as the raider from his team struggled to free himself from an opponent's grasp. He had been brought to the ground and his face was turning blue. According to the rules, he had to get back to his safety zone without taking a breath and

while chanting the game chant: *Kabaddi, Kabaddi, Kabaddi.*
But he couldn't do it. He finally had to take a breath and his
team lost that point.

Just beyond the Gul Mohr tree, I noticed something very
interesting. Ramu and Rukmani were standing together as
close as two slices of bread in a sandwich! I hid behind the
*Gul Mohr* and tried to hear the romantic rendezvous.

"Let me have a small…." That was Ramu mumbling.

"*Na*! Bring me a green mango first!" That was Rukmani
commanding.

"Please…" That was Ramu begging.

"*Tch*! First, a mango!"

"But my dearest Rukmani…"

She crossed her arms against her chest and turned
away from him.

What was going on? Why was Ramu pleading with
her so?

He bent down and rummaged for stones, then threw
them at the mango tree one by one, trying to knock down
some fruit. Every stone missed its mark by a mile. Poor
Ramu tried again and again.

Rukmani just stood by and laughed at him.

On the tenth try, he felled a mango for her. He ran to
pick it up, then approached Rukmani with his lips pursed.
Was he hoping for a kiss? I hugged the tree harder.

Rukmani snatched the mango away from Ramu's hand
before the poor fellow knew what was what.

"Oh Rukmani, do give us a small k…"

I watched them lean into each other. The pulse in my neck raced faster than a deer on the run. *Oo Ma!* Did this mean a black bead necklace for Rukmani's swan neck? Did this mean the Milk Boy was forgotten? I shifted to get a better position.

"*Oi!* What are you doing behind the Gul Mohr tree?" Paki demanded loudly.

The owls were back! I turned on my heel to run, but Rukmani's steely voice stopped me. "Not so fast, nimble-footed missy!"

*Arrey daiyya!* Thanks to the *goonda* boys, I'd been caught red-handed!

"She was spying again," Paki said to Rukmani.

"With both ears cocked in your direction!" Raju added.

"We were on our way to fly our kite and there she was hiding behind the tree with her *lengha* tucked between her legs!" Paki said.

"Oh ho! I have an earful for you, you scrawny thing!" Rukmani hissed.

I was really in for it! She'd rant and rave and call me all manner of names. There would be a great big storm in a tiny little teacup, thanks to the *goonda* boys, unless—unless I walked right up and threatened to tell Ramu about the *laddu* for the Milk Boy.

"Come here, spy!" Rukmani commanded.

I had two ways out of the mess. Either I could save my skin by lying just a little—*I was merely collecting an orange flower for your lovely black hair*—or I could stop her in her tracks by telling on her. But I wasn't entirely sure she'd care if Ramu knew or not.

But before I could do anything, Ramu stepped in. "Let the little one go, Rukmani," he said. "She meant no harm."

"She meant no harm? Are you a fool?" Rukmani asked, all the softness gone from her voice.

"She's definitely a spy *and* an eavesdropper!" Paki said.

"Yes, yes!" added Raju.

"She meant nothing by it," Ramu repeated, his words sharp and clear.

"*Aiyyo!*" sneered Rukmani. "What are you—a champion of the little spy girl?"

"*Bas*, Rukmani," Ramu snapped. "Enough!"

And with that, he silenced a tongue that usually wagged faster than Kalu's tail. He told the *goonda* boys to scram and when he turned to me, his voice was kind. "Go home, Basanta," he said.

I ran away as fast as I could. Dear, dear Ramu. He was not such a timid man after all. He was good and strong and brave and kind. God promise and mother promise and swear on my head, I'd never, never spy on him again!

# Chapter 18

The *goonda* boys were preparing for another kite battle. Paki waited for the wind to pick up a little. When the mango leaves began to rustle and coconut fronds swayed, he commanded Raju to walk the kite, nose up, a hundred feet upwind.

I watched Raju back away from him, farther and farther up the field, as Paki let out the line on the spool. *"Bas! Far enough!"* Paki shouted.

Raju held the kite skyward. It strained and trembled against the taut line.

*"Ub! Now!"* commanded Paki, and his brother thrust the kite upward and let go.

The wind caught the kite and lifted it up, up, up. Paki tightened the line and gave it slack, urging it skyward all the while.

*"Wah, Wah!"* Raju cheered. "Nice going, Big Brother!"

"According to Raju here, you've been looking high and low for the dumb dog," Paki said to me, his eyes glued on his kite. "Have you found him yet? Not that I care very much!"

"*Na*. I think Bala knows but he's not telling," I replied.

"Interesting you should say that."

"Interesting?"

"I saw Bala in the garbage bins the other day. 'What are you doing?' I asked. 'Searching for a bone,' he answered. 'Why?' I asked him. 'Mind your own business!' he said."

There it was! Bala *was* holding back and Paki had just confirmed my suspicion.

"You are an owl for not telling me about this sooner," I said. "You are a donkey and you are a liar."

"So are you!" Paki yelled. "You are an owl and a she-donkey and a spy and a liar too!"

"I am not!" I screamed.

At least I was not two of those things.

Lali and I decided to follow Bala and see if he led us to Kalu. We looked for him near Lalla-ji's store. We ran to the junk dealer's shack to see if he was lurking there. We checked at the bakery, where the smell of buns was sweet and warm, then the kite seller's shop, but we did not find him.

At last we spotted Bala quite by chance, his scruffy head a quick dancing dot in a rushing river of pedestrians, animals, carts, and vehicles. He walked purposefully, clutching a sugarcane in one hand. He bit off sugary chunks, chewed all the juice out, then spat the pulp in the road. In his other hand, he held a parcel.

"Let's go!" I said to Lali.

We dodged rickshaws and bicycles and carts to run after him, ducking quickly when he turned to look over his shoulder. It wouldn't do to be foiled in our pursuit.

"He's a cagey devil," I whispered. "See how he looks here and there as though he's got something to hide."

"Are you sure you know what you're doing?" panted Lali.

"Hush! No time for questions!" It didn't matter if I knew or not. I was operating on a hunch—a very good hunch.

Bala turned right at the bangle woman's shop, and we followed. He swerved at the beetle nut stand, and we swerved right behind him.

"He's heading for home," I whispered.

"What's he got in his other hand?" Lali asked.

"Something fishy," I said.

"Is it a clue?"

"It could be."

The plot was thickening like top cream in Ganga's milk pail. Surely we were close to something very big.

"I'm tired and my foot hurts," Lali said.

"Shhh!" I whispered. "It won't be long now."

We followed Bala out of the busy commercial streets and into the quieter alleyways where Amma said evil people snatched little children to cut off their hands and make them into beggars. But no one was lurking and no one was waiting to pounce. The alley was stinky but not sinister.

Lali and I pinched our noses, skirted open drains, and

jumped over cow droppings, dog poo, and rotting banana peels. We dodged wild cats, and hid behind posts where it smelled like piss and vomit. Tin-roofed shacks dotted a small clearing filled with a bunch of abandoned sewer pipes. Bala had led us to his home at last.

He lifted a limp rag that covered the doorway into a shanty and went inside. "Let's turn back," Lali said.

Turn back when we were *this* close? Was she joking?

"We're not going back," I told her.

"Okay. Now what?" Lali whispered.

"Now we wait," I replied.

"For what?"

"For...you know...something."

"Oh!"

We looked around for other clues but there were none. The shack had swallowed up Bala and there was nothing to see, nothing to hear, and nothing to do except wait.

"Let's go home," Lali begged again. "We shouldn't be in these parts in the first place."

I was beginning to think that maybe my hunch was wrong, but we were in too deep to turn back now. "I'm staying," I said firmly.

After what seemed like forever we heard a bark. *Bhaun! Bhaun!* Kalu approached the door of Bala's shack and waited obediently, his tail between his legs.

Before I could call to Kalu, Bala ducked out of his shanty, waving the mysterious parcel. "Here, Kalu. Here, good fellow!" he called.

Kalu went to Bala. He rubbed against his legs and looked at him with doleful eyes—the look he'd saved, till now, only for me!

"Good boy!" Bala stroked his head. "I've got fat bones for you, if you are good."

Kalu ran in a circle, chasing his tail. Bala snapped his fingers and Kalu jumped up and down, tongue lolling, then rolled on the ground.

"What's going on?" Lali asked.

I shushed her. I was trying to puzzle out the strange charade myself.

Bala dropped to his knees and curled his hands at his chest as if they were paws.

"He's gone mad," Lali whispered. "Don't you think?"

"He's too smart to go mad," I whispered back. "Bala is teaching Kalu to do tricks!"

"Tricks?"

Bala was waving a bone at Kalu now.

"See? He's using the bone as bait!" I explained.

"Huh?"

"Roll over for me," Bala said, "and there's another bone for you, Kalu my prince!"

Dutifully Kalu dropped and rolled. Bala gave him the bone.

"*Wah!* Bravo!" While the dog gnawed contentedly on his reward, Bala stroked his back. "One more bone for you, good dog, if you sit up and beg just the way I showed you."

Kalu sat up on his hindquarters and begged.

*"Shabaash!* Well done!"

I couldn't take it anymore. I stepped out from behind the pole. "Oh ho! I found you out, didn't I?"

Bala looked startled. "What are you doing here?" he demanded. "Are you spying?"

"Kalu!" I pointed an accusing finger. "You've had him all along."

"So what? What are you going to do about it?" Bala asked.

"You stole him!"

"Did not!"

"You did! You are a thief and a liar. You steal peanuts and dogs from other people and then turn around and lie about it without shame!"

"Kalu doesn't belong to anybody," Bala insisted. "And when you take something that belongs to no one, you're not stealing!"

"He has a point," Lali said.

"Rubbish!" I said. "Kalu is my friend! He comes to my house to eat and to sleep!"

"Not anymore!" Bala yelled. "He comes to me for food and he sleeps with me and he likes it very much!"

"What are you making him do?" Lali asked.

"I am teaching him tricks, if you must know," Bala growled.

"That we can see with our eyes!" I said. "And the main question is, *why?"*

"It's not your business!"

"I want to know!"

Bala threw his hands in the air. "So he can help me!"

"How can teaching him tricks help you, donkey?"

"So he can help me earn money, *okay*? Satisfied? Get out of here and leave us alone before I chuck a bone at you!"

I opened my mouth to yell again. But then I closed it quickly, because I understood. It all made perfect sense. I had seen trick monkeys turn somersaults many times. They wore funny hats and held tin cups in their hands and rang bells and beat on drums. The crowds laughed and threw coins. And the monkey's owner kept the coins.

"Come, Lali."

"Giving up so soon?" she asked.

"We're going home now." I tugged at her *lengha*.

"But, I don't understand," Lali said.

Bala held up another bone and Kalu jumped to his command.

"He's teaching him tricks," I explained. "People like tricks. They throw a lot of coins."

"You mean….?"

"Precisely."

"Oh," Lali said. "And you're going to let him keep Kalu?"

Yes, I was. It was what Amma would want me to do. Bala was right; Kalu had never belonged to me. He'd hung around because I offered him food and petted him; he paid me back by standing guard at my door. Now he was paying Bala back for the bones.

"Are you angry with Bala?" Lali asked.

I *was* angry. But I swallowed my anger. Plus this was exciting! A dog show was supremely exciting! He could have told me, though, and spared me so many hours of worry. Owl!

"Let's go tell Amma," I said. "I have a feeling she will be glad to know her darling boy has found something better than begging."

# Chapter 19

I lifted the curtain in Lali's doorway. "Lali, come! Let's go watch Kalu rehearse. Bala says he's learned all manner of tricks!" I said.

"*Na.* Hari is sick," she replied. "I must stay by his side." Lali stroked her little brother's forehead tenderly.

"Do come, Lali," I begged. "Nandi will stay with him. Look how soundly he sleeps. We'll be back well before he wakes up."

She thought about it for a minute, then agreed. "But I can't stay for long," she added.

On our way, we saw Paki in the jamun berry tree. "Come with us," I called. "We're going to watch Bala practice for the show."

"What show?" Paki asked.

"*What show?* Where have you been? Have you been living under a rock lately?"

"Kalu the Wonder Dog Show!" Lali explained. "Bala is going to make a pile of money from it!"

"Yeah, right!" Paki snorted.

"He is! It's as good as done!" I said.

"You're an idiot if you think he's going to pull it off," Paki said.

"He *is* going to pull it off and that's because he's smart—a thousand times smarter than a monkey on a branch of a jamun berry tree!" I shouted. "And what's more, Bala says you're a loser and the number one sissy boy this side of *Inglistan*. He's spreading the word this very moment!"

"What did you say?" Paki asked.

"Basanta, Basanta! What are you talking about, *hanh*?" Lali whispered.

"You heard me," I told Paki. "He says you are such a sissy chicken, you'd never climb up to the highest branch of the jamun berry tree in a million years!"

"Oh ho! He dares to say that?"

"Uh-huh. Those are his exact words."

"You're sweet on him, aren't you?" Paki asked. "That's it! Basanta the she-donkey is in love with Bala the he-donkey!"

"Shut up! Shut up!" I yelled.

"Are you coming or not?" Lali asked Paki.

"Not!" he shouted.

"Good!" I snapped. "It will be hard but we'll do our best not to cry!"

"Get out of here!" Paki yelled. "And tell your stupid boyfriend his stupid show is going to be a great big flop, flop, flop! You can tell him that came straight from the horse's mouth."

"Straight from a donkey's mouth," Lali said, and we left him in the jamun berry tree.

"Jump through the hoop," Bala begged the little dog. Big beads of perspiration rolled down his face and worry lines crisscrossed his forehead. "Jump, Kalu. Jump!" But Kalu only thumped his tail against the ground and yawned.

"*Oi*, Bala!" I hollered. "We hear there's going to be a dog show soon!"

"Can't you see I'm busy?" Bala growled.

"Don't mind us. Continue with your work," I told him. "We'll just watch."

"You're making Kalu nervous," Bala said.

"It's good practice to have an audience," I replied. "He needs to get used to it."

"Okay," Bala muttered. "But behave yourselves. You are warned!"

"We'll be quiet as mice," Lali promised.

Bala tried the hoop trick again. "*Aa*, Kalu," he commanded. "Come now!"

But the dog sank to the ground and lowered his head. Things weren't going so well for Bala today.

"Wave the bone, wave the bone!" I screeched so loudly that Kalu jumped up and scampered away, tail between his legs.

"Come back!" called Bala.

"Go back, go back!" cried Lali.

"The other way! That way!" I yelled.

With so much shouting going on, poor Kalu got all confused and darted about like a crazed mynah bird.

"The bone! The bone!" I hissed at Bala.

He ran into his shack and returned with a bone. "Come, Kalu!" he pleaded. Just as I knew it would, the bone got Kalu's attention.

"Now lower the hoop!" I shouted. "Lower it!"

Bala lowered the hoop a smidgen, took a deep breath, and waved the bone.

"Go for the bone, Kalu!" I called.

And this time, Kalu obeyed. He bounded forward and shot through the hoop like an arrow, clear to the other side.

"*Wah! Wah!* Bravo!" we cheered. "*Shabaash!* Well done! Long live Kalu! Long live Kalu!"

"That was brilliant, waving the bone and holding the hoop lower, *nai?*" I said to Bala.

"Yeah, I'm good!" He held his head high and puffed out his chest. "Just watch. I'll train my prince to turn around and jump right back!"

After they finished their practice, we ironed out the details, big and small, for the Wonder Dog Show. It were presented two days before *Divali*, when people would be caught up with the spirit of giving and wouldn't mind tossing a penny or two in the hat. We'd hang banners on Lalla-ji's storefront and on light posts. We'd get a fresh supply of bones from the butcher. I offered to bring a motia garland for Kalu and a hat too. How cute would that be?

People would come from near and far. After all, everyone loved a little bit of *shor* and *tamasha*—hullabaloo and spectacle. Didn't people always stop to watch the cobra fan its head? Didn't they always roar when a wicket got felled by the ball? It promised to be a number one, top-notch show, and the coins would make Bala a very rich boy!

"We should charge a fat commission," Lali said on our way back to our *busti*.

"Why, Lali!" I said. "You're turning into quite the businesswoman, don't you know!"

"I mean it. He's going to be raking in all that money with our help. We ought to get a cut of the profits."

"It never occurred to me to make him pay us," I said. "He really needs the money."

"I was just thinking that maybe a little share of the show money would keep the rice pot filled and buy medicine for Hari, that's all," Lali said softly.

How had I forgotten that the rice from Lalla-ji might be running low with payday still days away? I looked closely at my friend. Her eyes had lost their laughter and her lower lip trembled slightly. "Lali?"

"It's just that I have to find a way to get medicine for Hari. When I think about it now, I know it's mostly my fault he got sick."

"Don't be silly! Besides it's only a little cough," I said.

"It is my fault, don't you see?" Lali went on. "I let him

play in the water and I looked the other way when he ate tamarind. Amma told me to keep a good eye on him."

"You worry too much," I offered lamely.

"Now the cough is turning into a wheeze and—"

"Go! Go!" I said. "You're making a mountain out of a molehill!"

"I'm just saying a little money from the dog show profits would help, that's all," Lali said.

"Okay. You're right," I said. "I'll talk to Bala first thing tomorrow."

# Chapter 20

"Oi!" I hailed Bala on a Saturday morning.

"What? Back so soon?" he asked. It looked like he was teaching Kalu to run in and out of a make-shift obstacle course.

"I have another great idea for the dog show," I told him.

Bala gave Kalu's rump a brisk pat and walked over. "This better be good."

"We could get Dev and Pummi to do somersaults during the interval," I suggested.

"What?"

"I mean, you do want this to be a top-notch show, right?"

"Yes, but…"

"And as Kalu's owner, you ought to look good too. I brought you a comb so you could make your hair nice and slick for the big day."

"You've got to be kidding me! Is this some kind of joke?"

"Everything counts, don't you see?" I said. "I'm going to get Amma to sew a cute little cap for Kalu. Better than a paper hat. Now what do you think about that idea?"

"Hmm. *That* sounds pretty good."

"Precisely! And I was thinking I'd talk to Lalla-ji about donating puffed rice so we could sell it during halftime for some extra money."

Bala's eyes lit up. "Hey! That's not bad at all!"

"Do you hear the coins rolling in...*ding, ding, ding?*" I asked. "There are more ways to make the money grow!"

"Such as?"

I had him hook, line, and sinker by now. "Whoa! Not so fast," I said. "It's going to cost you. I mean, it's only fair."

We worked out all the details together. I asked for a fifty-fifty split, but Bala wouldn't hear of it. I tried to bargain with him, but he threatened to cut us out entirely if I kept bugging him.

In the end, I settled for 15 percent of the total take.

I was up in the guava tree plucking green fruit when I spied Paki and Raju.

"I'll teach that rascal!" Paki shook his fist. "I'll make him pay so dearly, he'll wish he'd never been born!"

"What will you do, Big Brother?" Raju asked.

I couldn't hear Paki's response, but I had a hunch that a wicked plan was being cooked up against Bala, on account of the fib I had made up about him yesterday. When Raju ran off in one direction and Paki took off in another, I jumped down. That owl Paki was up to something and I was going to find out exactly what.

I followed him as he weaved around the huts and headed toward the field. Halfway across the field, he turned toward the Milk Boy's house, then skirted it and sped to the back. He was going to the buffalo house! I picked up my skirt and ran faster but he'd already disappeared inside by the time I got there.

I stole close to the entrance and hid behind a nearby wheelbarrow. I strained to hear the mumblings coming from within, but it was no good—I could neither hear nor see. I abandoned my hiding place and darted to the easterly wall. Perhaps there I'd find a better vantage point. I saw a small window halfway up the wall; a wooden ladder lay nearby. With the quietest of grunts I propped the ladder against the wall and climbed up to press my nose to the window. The pane was dirty and the room dimly lit, but I could still see inside.

The Milk Boy was milking a buffalo, the brass pail tucked between his knees.

"Ganga, dear fellow." Paki slapped his back. "Hard at work just as I suspected. I came to see if you could use a hand."

The buffalo turned her head to look at him. In the other stalls, the other buffalo scraped at the straw with their hooves and let out mournful bellows from time to time.

"That's generous of you, Paki, b-b-but I can manage

on my own. My b-b-buffalo get skitterish with strangers near," Ganga said.

Paki leaned against the mud wall, crossed his legs, and chewed on a stalk of straw. "No worries! I am quiet as a mouse. No...even better! I am practically invisible, my man!"

Ganga's hands didn't break rhythm and the milk frothed in his pail.

Paki cleared his throat. "I hear you've got yourself another nice stash of firecrackers for *Divali* this year."

The buffalo stamped her hooves. "Ho...ho," Ganga murmured as he rubbed her flank to soothe her. "Father was generous," he said to Paki.

"He bought you...what, some twenty firecrackers or so?" Paki asked.

"It's a fair assortment," Ganga replied.

"Hmm. Well, well! Your father is large-hearted, *nai?*"

Ganga nodded. "He's thinking of giving B-B-Bala prize money for winning the kite b-b-battle."

Paki stood up straighter. "Say what?

"*Hanh.* He says the b-b-boy has a lot of potential and he's going to sponsor him. He admires his c-c-competitive spirit."

"He does now, does he?" Paki snapped. "Well, bless the man!" He kicked up a wad of straw and it landed near the buffalo's nose. She raised her head and emitted a bellow, which was met with answering calls from the adjacent stalls.

"Ho...ho," the Milk Boy said, patting the buffalo's side.

Paki shifted his weight from one leg to the other. "Back to firecrackers. Surely, my friend, you know your firecrackers were the talk of the *busti* last year? *Wah!* What magnificence! What power!"

"Lali told me she enjoyed them."

"Yes, yes. Not so long ago she said, 'My Ganga is so clever, he knows to pick the right ones—the ones that make the most noise.'"

Ganga reddened a little. *"Hanh.* The new ones are guaranteed to send the chickens fluttering and the dogs running a mile."

Paki went on. "She also said, 'My dear Ganga is so very clever. He keeps his firecrackers hidden from thieves in his father's steel trunk.'"

*"Na.* The dear girl is wrong." Ganga chuckled. "I keep them in a b-b-box b-b-behind the b-b-bale of hay."

At that, Paki bolted out of the buffalo house without so much as a backward glance. He was mumbling something, but I couldn't quite hear him over the buffalo's bellow. I thought I heard the word "Kalu," but I couldn't be sure.

I stood atop the ladder, trying to puzzle out what had just occurred. Paki had seemed nice enough, offering to help Ganga with the milking, but all that talk about the firecrackers...there had to be something going on with that. I climbed down and headed homeward, hoping my sleuthing hadn't been a great big waste of time.

# Chapter 21

**M**emsaab had some extra chores lined up for us, so Amma, Durga, and I left for work earlier than usual the next morning. We crossed the field and headed toward the jamun berry tree. As we neared, the leaves began to shake violently and *thock! thock! thock!* berries dropped down all around the trunk.

"They're in it again," I observed. "Just like two *jungli* monkeys without tails!"

"*Tch*," Amma muttered.

The rain of purple berries began to thicken. The rustling quickened, followed by a rattling and juddering of the branches. And then came a shrill cry from above—*Aaaaaa!*—and someone tumbled to the ground!

"Amma! Paki's fallen from the tree!" I screamed. I gathered up my skirt and ran. Amma followed, Durga bouncing on her hip.

Raju met us, flailing his arms and hollering. "Big Brother said he was going to the top! He said no one could stop him! He...*waaaah!*"

Paki lay motionless on the ground.

Amma peered closely into his face. "Paki?" she whispered. "Paki, my boy?"

"Is he dead?" My voice was shaking.

Paki stirred. "Ow! Ow!" he moaned. He opened his eyes and looked about like a wild animal.

"He's alive!" I cried.

"My leg!" groaned Paki. "My leg!"

"Hush! Lie still," Amma said. She held him down and prodded and probed him gently all over. She lifted his leg. "Do you feel this, my boy? Can you move your foot?"

Paki screamed and fought to get up.

Amma turned to Raju. "How high was he?"

"He fell from up there." He pointed.

I followed Raju's finger to the crook of the lower branches. The owl had not reached the top yet!

"He said he was going to show everyone he was the best climber this side of *Inglistan*," Raju bawled.

"It's not his head or his neck," Amma pronounced. "It's only his ankle. He's going to be *theek thaak*." At once she was all business. "Go find Ramu and tell him to bring his rickshaw," she said to Raju.

Paki had been up in the tree because of the big lie I had told him. He could have died. I could see it: people shaking their heads, clucking their tongues, grilling me, peppering me with questions. And Paki...poor Paki, lying still and silent under a shroud and a pile of marigolds. My stomach tied itself in knots.

"Are you okay, Paki?" I asked. "How many fingers am I holding up?"

"Give him room." Amma shoved me aside. "You'll be fit as a fiddle in a matter of days," she assured Paki, but he continued to scream.

Raju soon returned, his mother at his heels. Ramu was right behind them, pumping the rickshaw pedals as fast as he could.

"*Aiyyo!*" wailed the washerwoman. "One hundred times I have told the boy to stay away from that tree! One thousand times! *Aiyyo! Aiyyo!*"

"Never mind that!" Amma snapped. "You must take him to the Doctor Babu."

But the washerwoman beat her chest. "*Aiyyo*, sister!" she wailed. "How will I do that? This boy spent my spare change on his precious kites last week!" To Ramu she said, "Brother, I will be beholden to you if you will take him to my home."

Ramu picked Paki up and gently carried him to the rickshaw. He pedaled away, the washerwoman and Raju running alongside.

"Tie a poultice around his ankle when you get him home!" Amma called.

"Is he going to be all right?" I asked. "Is he going to be lame for the rest of his life?"

"It was a close call," she replied somberly. "But, yes, the boy is going to be fine. And no, if Lord Rama wills it, he will not be lame for the rest of his life."

I couldn't keep my mind on my chores at the Big House, and Amma got angry with me for getting in her way. "He's going to be just fine," she said. She didn't know that I had other things on my mind in addition to Paki's ankle.

I felt like everything was spinning out of control. Little Hari was burning up with fever, Vimla Mausi and Lali were sick with worry, and Mausi's payday had not yet arrived. I had lied to Paki about Bala, and there was no telling what Rukmani would have to say about the *laddu* for Ganga. And now Paki had fallen from the tree, and it was all my fault.

I was so wrapped up in my thoughts that Little Bibi had to yell in my ear to get my attention. "There were a million mosquitoes in my bed last night and they bit me half to death!" she shouted.

"Yes, Little Bibi?"

"Hello? Mosquitoes? See?" She thrust out an arm covered in prickly red welts.

*Aiyyo!* I'd tried hard! I had. I'd slapped away the mosquitoes and when I let the netting drop, I swear there wasn't a single insect in the bed. I brushed away a tear. There were so many bigger things happening and Little Bibi was worried about a few measly mosquito bites?

"Why are you sniffling?" she asked.

I wiped my eyes quickly with the back of my hand.

Oh, where to begin? "The washerwoman's boy fell from the jamun berry tree, Bibi," I said. My tears burst out like water from a broken jug.

"Paki? Pentamma's boy? Why didn't she come to Mama about it right away?"

My mistress expected an answer but I had nothing for her but more sniffles.

I felt Little Bibi's arm around my shoulder, followed by a kind squeeze. "Wait here," she said. She went to her cupboard and came back with a big wad of rupees. "It's my pocket money," she continued. "Give it to him."

My eyes widened at the money. There was enough there to pay for a visit to the Doctor Babu.

"For heaven's sake, you're not going to cry again, are you?" Little Bibi said, but this time her voice was a mixture of stern and kind. It was a good voice.

"Cry, Little Bibi? Oh no! I am smiling, see?" I showed Little Bibi all my perfectly straight, pearly white teeth that I cleaned each morning with the twig of the bitter neem tree until they sparkled like the insides of seashells.

I lifted the threadbare curtain. The hut was silent. I could see Paki curled up in a darkened, smoky corner. "Pentamma Mausi?" I whispered, not wanting to wake him. "Raju?"

But their mother was not there, nor was Raju.

Paki stirred. I tried ducking away but his sleepy voice stopped me at the doorway. *"Oi!* Why are you hollering like a headless rooster?" He rubbed his eyes.

I drew closer. A hazy ray streamed through the opening in the wall and fell on his face, showing sleep lines as deep as the creases in my *lengha*. "It was not a holler, Paki, it was a whisper," I said.

"If that's a whisper, I am a monkey's uncle." Paki hobbled off the mat. "It woke me up, didn't it?"

"I came to see how you were."

"Bravo! A regular do-gooder!"

I swallowed hard. I didn't blame him for being angry. If our positions were reversed, I'd be hopping mad too. "I didn't mean for you to fall out of the tree," I said.

"Liar! It was exactly what you intended. You probably jumped for joy, didn't you?"

"Does your leg hurt terribly?"

*"Does your leg hurt terribly?"* Paki echoed me mockingly. "What do you think? Of course it hurts, you she-donkey! It hurts very much!"

"I am sorry, Paki, I truly am."

"A fat lot of good that does me!" Paki barked. "And now I have all this pain for nothing!"

"What do you mean?"

"Bala denied everything! 'What, me?' he asked. *'Na baba!* Basanta lied to you.'"

So the truth was out!

"You are a liar and a spy and a spreader of malicious gossip!" Paki said.

"I couldn't help it," I said, truly sorry. "One thing just led to the other."

"Go! Go! Everyone can help what they do!"

The owl had a point, but was this not a question of a pot calling the kettle black?

The jute curtain flapped and Pentamma Mausi came in. "*Aiyyo,* Paki! I told you one hundred times to lie still."

"I was doing that, Amma. I was lying as still as a mouse when—"

"There you are, Pentamma Mausi," I said, turning in relief. "I came to see how Paki was doing."

"The poultice around his leg would help it heal if he would not bounce around like mung beans in a pot," she told me.

I held out the money for her.

"*Arrey daiyya!* What is this?" Pentamma Mausi asked.

"It's from Little Bibi for the Doctor Babu," I explained.

"You approached the Big House for us?" Pentamma Mausi cupped my chin with her hand. "Your heart is as big as the sky, dear child. It comes to you from your mother, *nai?*"

Pentamma Mausi counted out all the rupees, folded them into a corner of her *pullo,* and tied them in a secure knot.

# Chapter 22

Hari coughed so hard that he sounded like a loco-
motive. Vimla Mausi sat on her pallet, crying
quietly. Amma had sent me with another box of
food, but I found myself wishing I had also held back some
of Little Bibi's money for Lali.

I shook the thought out of my head. To each his own
kismet, Amma would say. Little Bibi's money was for Paki.
Vimla Mausi's better time lay ahead, and surely there'd be
something good in her destiny too.

I untied the cloth and emptied the tiffin box into a
rimmed platter. "Look! It's *dhal* and *gawar* beans. Mmmm!"

Nandi, Pummi, and Dev came running. Lali helped me
spoon out the food and the little ones gobbled it down.

"I don't want Hari to die like my father." Lali looked so
scared that I put my arm around her neck.

"Eat, Lali," I coaxed. "If your stomach is full you will
feel so much better."

She took a few small bites and then we went to sit under
the tamarind tree. The sun was setting. Around us, dust
was beginning to whirl.

"What are you thinking, Lali?" I asked. She had a far-away look in her eyes.

"Sometimes I think to myself…if I had proper feet like Basanta, I'd earn a proper wage like she does," she said.

"Don't be silly," I said. "Who'd look after the little ones?"

"Nandi would. She's old enough and she's responsible. The extra money would help. It would!"

"You shouldn't worry so," I said. "Hari is going to get better, you'll see."

"I'm not so sure," Lali said with a sob. "I had a bad dream last night. I saw Hari on a cloud, drifting away… farther and farther until he was a tiny speck. And then I could see him no longer. It's a bad omen."

"Rubbish!" I scolded. "You've got Paki's kites on your mind!" But I was worried too. I eased the ring off my finger. "Take it, Lali," I said. "Your mother can sell it for medicine." I pressed the ring into her hand.

Lali pulled away, refusing the ring with a shake of her head. "It's for your trousseau," she insisted. She wouldn't take it, no matter what I said, so I changed the subject and told her about the deal I had made.

Lali's eyes lit up a little. "You spoke to Bala?"

"I went to him straightaway."

"And he agreed to a whole 15 percent?"

"After a wee bit of arm twisting. It's not much, but it's better than nothing."

"You're right," Lali said. "There's only one thing. The dog show's not until next week. I can't wait that long."

She had a point. For once, I had nothing to say.

The wind began to pick up and dark clouds rolled in from the west.

"Rain will help to cool things down," I mused. And yet I knew it might just be a trick. Sometimes all the thunderclaps and lightning flashes and wind bursts amounted to nothing more than a noisy spectacle.

But the wind grew stronger and dust swirled around us like a giddy child spinning on her heel. Debris stung our arms and tamarind leaves flew into our noses. I shielded my eyes as branches shook and twigs rained around us.

"It's a big one," Lali said, looking skyward. "Ganga's buffalo are probably getting skitterish."

"You'll be rich when you marry him," I said. "He may be a simpleton but he is kind and will make you happy."

*Whoosh!* A fierce gust blew my *lengha* above my knees. I could hear Amma calling me in. But I wanted to stay a little longer.

"Ba-saaan-taaa!" Amma's voice came again, more urgently this time.

Lali tugged at my *lengha*. "Do you hear? Mausi's calling. We better go now."

"Not yet." I shook my head. A brilliant idea had just come to me. Lali's kismet was about to change!

# Chapter 23

The wind had died down as quickly as it had begun. The clouds had all been chased away, and the sky was blue once more. Yesterday's storm had been a trick after all. But we were glad for the sunshine. It would help us do our job today.

Lali and I sat under the guava tree, surrounded by pots, big and small. They were filled with the tamarind pods we had collected yesterday after the wind knocked them down from the tree.

"Tell me again," Lali said. "Why exactly are we are doing all this big work?"

"Goose!" I laughed. "This big work's going to earn us big money for Mausi."

"But it's going to take us hours and hours..."

"Tell me, Lali. Are you afraid of hard work?"

Lali shook her head. *"Na!"* she said. "I'm not afraid."

"Good! I'm not either!" I was used to working hard for Little Bibi, all week long. It wasn't so much more to do a bit extra for a friend.

We rolled up our sleeves and got busy. First we cracked

the brown tamarind pods open with our thumbs to remove the pulpy fruit. Next we soaked the fruit in water until it was soft and squishy. Then we held a bunch of the fruit in our hands and pressed. The dark brown pulp oozed out between our fingers and dripped into a pot. We saved the seeds that were trapped in our palms to add to our stash later.

We stirred sugar and salt and cumin and red chili powder into the pulp. Amma had agreed to let us have them after we told her what we were doing. "*Daiyya!* Such curious notions!" she grumbled, but she gave us a little bit of everything we needed.

We scooped globs of tamarind out onto a palm frond mat, stuck a small stick into each glob, and set the mat in the blazing sun for the candy to dry. We worked late into the afternoon, until our backs ached and our palms were as wrinkled as Old Nahni's face.

When they were done, we had a pile of mouth-puckering, eye-crinkling tamarind lollipops to sell to the people of the *busti,* ten paisa a piece.

"We're going to have ourselves the best tamarind candy sale ever!" I told Lali.

But she was not convinced. "It may not work."

"What may not work?"

"This!" Lali swept her hand at the growing mound of candy. "We've worked until our arms are sore, but people may not come."

"They'll come," I reassured her.

They *would* come. Who in their right mind would say no to a mouthwatering tamarind lolly? Still, to be safe we recruited Nandi and Pummi to get the word out.

The sun burned down mercilessly.

*"Oo Maa!"* Lali fanned herself with the hem of her skirt.

For once I was glad for the heat. "Look, Lali!" I tested a lolly with my fingertip. "The hot sun is already drying them up nicely!"

We shooed away flies. We talked about this and that. We waited and waited under the guava tree.

*"Na.* No one's coming," Lali said.

The *busti* was quiet. Where was Ramu? Rukmani? The old cobbler? Where were Paki and Raju?

I stared at the piles of lollies. "Maybe the heat is keeping everyone indoors," I said. "Paki and Raju should have been the first ones, though. We all know how they are about the tamarind—"

"Paki's not coming," Lali said.

"He is!" I insisted. "He loves tamarind second only to his kites!"

"He can't walk this far yet," Lali reminded me.

*Oo Maa!* All the hard work and exciting thoughts had made me forget about Paki's leg. But still, he hadn't been crying so much in the hut, and two days had passed since his fall.

We waited, but no one came. My head was full of troubling thoughts. Then we heard loud squeals and Nandi and Pummi came flying toward us.

"*Oi!*" Nandi squawked. "Prepare yourself!"

Following them was a crowd of people!

"They're here!" I yelled to Lali. "I told you they'd come!"

Raju was the first in line with money in his fist.

"How's Paki feeling?" I asked.

"Better, not that it's your business," Raju snarled. "He begged Amma to let him come, but she threatened him with a thrashing. Doctor Babu said he'll soon be as good as new. Our mother was so happy, she gave me extra to spend."

"Yes, yes," I said. "You must buy many."

"*Oi!*" Raju pointed to the fattest ones. "Let us have that one...and the one over there!"

Business was brisk and coins rained into our bowls! The sugarcane man bought some, and so did the peanut man. The bangle woman came running, and the maker of palm frond baskets as well. We sold to the vegetable vendor and to the seller of beetle nut leaves.

Even Amma dug pennies out from the knot in her *pullo*. "There's a child lurking in everyone," she laughed as she licked her lollipop.

"I wish Vimla Mausi were here to share in the fun," I said.

"She keeps close to Hari," Amma replied. "A mother can be only as happy as her saddest child," she murmured. "Sister Vimla's time for happiness may not be today but if Lord Rama wills it, it will surely come tomorrow."

*We can't wait that long,* I said to myself.

The lollies ran out about the time the sun went down, and everyone went home feeling satisfied. Lali and I scooped up our earnings, threw them in the air, and laughed at the tinkling shower of coins. The pile was so big that it filled three pouches to the brim. Our throats were raw and our voices were hoarse from eating so many tart lollies, but our hearts were happy.

I made Lali swear on her head that she wouldn't breathe a word to her mother. The lollies were my idea and I wanted to be the one to tell her.

Their hut was so dark that I could barely discern the hump that was Vimla Mausi's *chullah*. A small fire was burning in the fat, round stove. Poor Hari lay still on a mat, his face to the wall. His breath came out in short rasps.

"How's he doing today?" I asked Mausi.

"He has kept down a few bites of soft rice," she replied.

"You were right about the dream," Lali told me. "He is a little more spirited and that's a good thing, *nai?*"

"He probably still needs the Doctor Babu," I said, thrusting the money into Mausi's hand.

Her eyes widened.

"It's for proper medicine," Lali said.

"*Arrey daiyya!* Did your dear and generous mother send this?" Mausi asked.

I shook my head. I told her about the tamarind lollipop sale from start to finish and Lali filled in the details.

Vimla Mausi's fist closed over the money. I could tell by the glistening in her eyes that she was very happy and very relieved.

There was nothing left for me to do. "I'll be going then." I folded my hands in respectful parting.

Mausi stopped me with a kiss on my forehead. "Your heart is better than gold, dear child," she said. "Your mother has reared you well."

# Chapter 24

It took me two days to get my voice back. Little Bibi said I sounded cute, and that made me so happy that I hummed all day. I made extra sure that there were no mosquitoes in her bed netting.

That evening, as I made my way to the dear tamarind tree, the strong smell of coconut oil assailed my nose. Rukmani sat under the mango tree, oiling her hair.

"*Oi!* Come sit with me for a bit of chitchat," she called in a lazy voice. She was humming and I took that as a good sign. I walked up to her.

"*Arrey*, Basanta!" Rukmani drawled. "I am so bored I could scream. Tell me stories of the Big House, *nai?*"

I was startled by her request. I'd been prepared for an earful about hiding behind the Gul Mohr tree or about the failed *laddu* mission, but the flighty girl appeared to have moved on to newer ground.

She was asking about something that was clearly out of bounds, though. "Do not discuss Memsaab and Big Master and Little Bibi with anyone," Amma had warned me time and time again. "They are not the business of others."

"There's nothing to tell. Everything is just ho-hum," I told Rukmani.

"That's not my impression." She coiled her hair into a tight bun with an expert twist of her wrist. "If I were to go by the size of the Big House, I'd say you get no respite from horrible Little Bibi's demands on you, you poor sorry little scrawny thing."

Was Rukmani feeling sorry for me? Or was she only rubbing it in? "My job's not so bad," I said. "And Little Bibi—"

"And Little Bibi, what? Tell, tell, *nai?*"

"Little Bibi's fine," I declared. "She's actually quite nice and helpful."

"*Oo Ma!*" Rukmani curved a finger under her nose to signify her skepticism. "Just listen to you, sticking up for precious Little Bibi!"

"I'm not!" I said. But I *had* jumped to Little Bibi's defense. I had done for my young mistress what Ramu had done for me.

"These hoity-toity rich folk!" Rukmani sneered. "*Oo Ma!* So many stories... Would you like to hear about my *memsaab?*"

"*Hanh!* Of course I would." Amma had strict instructions about talking about *my memsaab* but she had no rules about others.

"My *memsaab* has little bottles with water that smells so nice."

"It's called *scent.*" I knew I sounded haughty, but I kept talking. "It's an *Angrezi* or *Eengleesh* word, as Little Bibi would say. She has rows and rows of pretty bottles on her dressing table."

"*Aiyyo!* I know *Angrezi* too, Miss Show-off!" Rukmani snapped. "I know all about scent too, and I will let you sniff. Come!"

She extended her wrist and I got a whiff of rose petals and jasmine.

"And this...look!" She tilted back her head. Tucked behind her *pullo,* nestled in her bosom, was a delicate string of black beads.

"Where did you get those?" I asked.

"*Aiyyo!* No need to look so shocked," Rukmani said scornfully. "It's not like you've never taken a thing or two!"

"Never mind," I said. "I've got something for you."

"Oh?"

"It's a sweet message from a sweet man!"

By now, Ramu's message was very old, but I had promised him that I would tell her. *Shame, shame!* I chided myself, and then, to make myself feel better, I added, *Perhaps he's already whispered it in her ear under the mango tree.*

"He said to tell you he's saving to buy a cozy little house on the other end of town."

"Oh, he did, did he?"

"Yes...a nice house for the girl with a swan walk. Those are his words!"

"*Humph!* Tell me something I don't already know!"

*Arrey daiyya!* Ramu *had* told her! "Will there be a wedding in the *busti* this year?" I asked.

"Wouldn't you just love to know?" Rukmani tossed a green guava in the air and caught it with a snap. "Run along," she said dismissively. "Tell your little friend all the latest gossip, and while you're at it, you might tell Ramu I will not wait forever."

I turned to go and then stopped. There was something I had been meaning to clear up. "Oh, Rukmani," I said. "About that night..."

There was a sharp intake of breath. "What night?"

"The night Kalu barked when someone tried to steal our stuff?"

"*Aiyyo!* So?"

"My father says he has a fair idea who the thief is, and if she dares try again, he'll go straightaway to the police station."

Rukmani flinched. "*Aiyyo!* Why are you telling me all this?"

"No reason."

"It's no skin off my nose. I don't care what your father says!" Rukmani turned on her heel and walked away really fast, her hips swaying with a *thumak, thumak.*

My hunch had been right! The nervous glances, twitches, and tics were proof that Rukmani had tried to steal the ring.

"Wait!" I yelled. "I'm going to make a garland of motia flowers for your pretty neck if there is a wedding."

But she didn't even look back.

# Chapter 25

The excitement was building for the Festival of Lights. My neighbors were readying oil lamps, refreshing *rangoli* patterns, and hanging mango-leaf runners. Memsaab had us scrubbing and scouring the Big House, and the grocery list for the Big Kitchen was a yard long.

Amma and I sipped our late morning tea during our break. She wrapped the end of her *pullo* around the rim of her brass tumbler and I used a kitchen rag to keep my fingers from getting burned.

I took a big slurp.

"So much noise!" Amma chided gently. "You sound like monsoon thunder."

The floor was cool under my thin cotton *lengha* and when I ran a finger along the stone slab, there was hardly a speck of dust on it. I watched the ants shimmying under the pantry door to get to the sugar.

The little packet in my *choli* was growing warm from the touch of my skin. Earlier, I had sifted through my treasure box and chosen with care. There was one less thing in it now. The best thing I owned was hiding in my *choli*, and that was because *Divali* was a day for giving.

"A penny for your thoughts," Amma said.

"I was wondering if Little Bibi will give me a *Divali* gift this year."

"Why should this year be different?" Amma asked.

*The ring*, I thought. *She might skip this year because of that.*

"It's the ring, isn't it?" Amma asked, reading my mind.

I sucked in my breath. "Yes. That's what I was thinking."

"It's an old story, *nai?*" Amma said gently, and she was right. Things had moved on. Little Bibi's new ring was on her third finger and the old ring with the missing stone was on mine.

"But I still remember the way she looked at me the day the ring went missing, Amma," I said.

"Your imagination, nothing more!" Amma said. "Her tongue is sharp but her heart is big. She absolved you in clear words. Is that not enough?"

But a voice kept chiding me with these words: *Evil girl! You took the ring! You kept it! This is why there might not be a gift for you.*

Amma cupped my chin in her hand. "Let it go, child," she said.

I nodded. I *was* letting Little Bibi's eyes bruise my heart too much. That was making me forget her goodness again and again. It was not exactly fair to her. Lately, Little Bibi had been kind and nice. Still, I envied my young mistress her riches. I envied her the power of giving. "It's nice to have a pile of money isn't it?" I asked.

"Hmm?"

"I mean…you can give away a lot when you have a lot."

"Not entirely true." Amma blew in her tea. "The only ingredient needed is a big heart."

We tipped our tumblers and drained our tea. Amma pushed herself off the floor. "There's much good in giving," she said. "What will you give our Little Mistress for *Divali*?"

"I already give more than I get."

"Oh?"

"What about those glasses of water she makes me fetch and those comfortable nights she enjoys with no mosquitoes to bother her?"

"*Daiyya!*" Amma smiled. "I forgot about those things."

The rooster crowed in the yard and the gong of the clock tower rolled in over the compound wall.

"*Aiyyo!*" clucked Amma. "Already so late, and so much left to do." She went to the hearth to stoke the fire and I dusted off my *lengha*. I too had plenty to do.

"I'll sweep in the Big House now," I said, reaching for the broom.

The midday sun had driven the hens into the coop; the sparrows and crows were silent too. I threaded a garland in the shade of the motia bush, and waited for Little Bibi to return from school.

I plucked the flowers one by one. The motia released its sweet smell and my hands were soon perfumed with it. I held the blossoms to my nose and inhaled deeply. Sometimes, when the nights were unbearable, I'd place a cluster of motia close to my nose and let the fragrance slice through the heat like a knife in warm butter.

My head began to droop and my eyelids grew heavy, but each new rattle and creak made me straighten up with a start. Had my mistress come home at last?

I heard the groan of the Big Gate and my pulse quickened. Before I could stand or even take one step, Little Bibi called for me. "Basanta!"

I ran to her room, then paused in the doorway.

"Come here," Little Bibi commanded.

My eyes widened at the parcel in her hand. *Oo Maa!* Little Bibi hadn't forgotten after all! "For me, Little Bibi?"

"Open it!" she said with a smile.

My new red and green *Divali* dress was as lovely and soft as a baby chick! Little Bibi also gave me matching slippers!

And she gave me a book. My heart skipped a beat— didn't she know I couldn't read? I must have looked confused because Little Bibi announced that my reading lessons would begin soon! I was so happy I almost forgot that I had something for her too.

"Little Bibi? I have a gift for you," I said with a grin. And from my *choli*, I pulled out her present.

"What's this?" Little Bibi stared at my hand.

"Why, Little Bibi, it's a piece of mica...the largest and clearest one I've found so far!"

"What does one do with it?"

*What does one do with it?* I hardly knew what to say.

"Why, Bibi, so many things...." I dug into my little pocket quickly for the string of flowers. "And I made this for your hair!"

Little Bibi smiled when she saw the flowers. "Yes, this I like a lot." She pinned the motia near her right ear. "Well? How do I look?"

"So pretty, Bibi. Truly!"

"I'll take the flowers," Little Bibi said. "But you can keep the mica."

I felt like a deflated balloon. How could she refuse the mica? It was the best thing in my treasure box! It was a special gift without a single hole or imperfection!

"It's very pretty when the sunlight streams through it, Little Bibi," I said.

"You don't say!" Little Bibi chuckled, but she still gave it back.

She should have kept it. It was a gift.

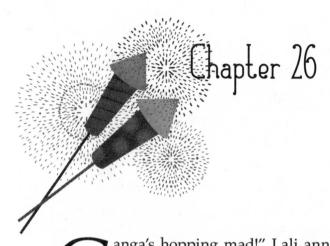

# Chapter 26

"G anga's hopping mad!" Lali announced when she met me at the tamarind tree.

I arched my brow. Ganga was a placid boy. He never shouted or screamed, even when the buffalo kicked over the milk pail.

"Paki stole his best firecrackers from behind the bale of hay," she told me. "He had twenty at the last count, and now he has only eight!"

"Go! Go!"

"It's true. And he knows Paki's the one."

"How can he be sure?"

"He put two and two together, that's how. Paki came to the buffalo house to ask one hundred questions about the firecrackers and now the best of the lot are missing!"

"The best of the lot?"

"*Hanh*. The ones that can make chickens flutter and flap and dogs run a mile!"

"Why would Paki take them? He's already got a stash of sparklers saved up for *Divali*."

"Sparklers are not firecrackers. But there's more to it,"

Lali went on. "Before he left, Paki told my Ganga something that set off an alarm in his clever head."

"An alarm?"

"*Ding! Ding!* He said Bala was going to be sorry he got born at all, and so was Kalu."

"Bala? Kalu? Wait a minute...what do they have to do with the missing firecrackers?"

"Don't you see the connection?" Lali asked.

I thought about it for a moment and then my eyes widened. "You mean...?"

"Exactly!" Lali nodded. "And Ganga agrees. So devious, *nai?*"

"It makes perfect sense, Lali!" I cried. "I heard him muttering when I tailed him to the buffalo house and I thought I heard him say something about Kalu! I witnessed everything from the ladder. Oh ho! That tricky rascal went back for Ganga's fireworks behind the bale of hay with a wicked purpose in mind!"

*Oo Maa!* Paki was planning to sabotage the Wonder Dog Show! Now that he was back on his feet, he'd use the firecrackers to scare Kalu and leave Bala high and dry. *Daiyya re daiyya!* Paki's scheme was leading straight back to mine. Still, Ganga was a silly blabbermouth.

"Ganga should have known better!" I said. "He's a number one fool for giving away his hiding spot!"

Lali stamped her good foot. "He's not! He's kind and clever. He's the one who put two and two together!"

"A fat lot of good that does Bala now!"

There was no time to quibble over the Milk Boy's good and bad points. The Wonder Dog Show was two days away and there was absolutely no time to lose! We ran to the buffalo shed.

Ganga walked up to us with a flower in his hand, a message of love in his eyes, and a puppy-dog smile for his dear girl on his lips.

"The flower can wait, Ganga." I pushed his hand away from Lali's left ear. "We've got plenty more important things to worry about right now!"

The three of us huddled behind the hay bales to form our counterplot.

"Ganga will sneak into Paki's hut and steal them back," I proposed, but Lali put her foot down.

"Ganga is not a thief," she said. "He is good and kind!"

"Perhaps w-w-we should go to Paki's mother or c-c-confront him directly," Ganga ventured.

"Don't be an idiot, Ganga!" I snapped. "He'd just deny it!"

"You don't have to be so mean," Lali grumbled. "Ganga's only trying to help."

We finally settled on plan number 4, shook on it, and went our separate ways.

The day of the Wonder Dog Show, I ran around in circles like a headless chicken. The clock in the station tower had struck nine; the show was only two hours away and there wasn't a lot of time left for our mission.

At exactly half past nine, Lali and I went to Paki's hut.

"Paki! Oh Paki!" we called, but he didn't answer.

"Do you suppose he's in the field already?" I whispered. All would be lost if that were true!

"The show's not until eleven o'clock," Lali said. "He'd be a fool to make himself conspicuous by being there too early, *nai?*"

"He might be in the jamun berry tree."

"*Na.* His mother would kill him for sure!"

"You are right," I said. "Let's yell louder."

"Paki! Oh Paki!"

And this time, Paki came out with a big scowl on his face. I eyed the suspicious bulge in his pocket and exchanged a knowing look with Lali. *Oh ho,* our eyes said. *What do you suppose is hiding there?*

"What do you want?" Paki demanded. "Better get on with it. I have important things to do today."

"Your foot's mended nicely, thanks to the good Lord Rama," Lali said sweetly.

"No thanks to Miss Destruction here." Paki glowered at me. He had apparently forgotten that I had played a pretty big part in helping his foot mend.

"We have an important message from the Milk Man," I said. "Something about a handsome reward for you."

Paki was all ears. "What reward?"

"Oh, a consolation prize for the kite war."

"Hmm. I've been told about a reward for the winner," Paki said.

"*Oh ho!* Who told you?"

"Never mind, nosy girl! You say there's a consolation prize too?"

"*Hanh!* I believe it's a large cash prize to keep the competitive spirit going. Sounds mighty suspicious, if you ask me."

"A large cash prize?"

Paki had taken the bait.

"A great big one!" Lali said.

"And oh yeah...one more thing," I told him. "You are to go right away to the buffalo shed because he said it's a one-time deal, a take-it-or-leave-it kind of offer."

"Did he say how much money?"

"Not exactly, but it's a bundle, I'm guessing," I said. "Ganga said something about it being enough to buy a lifetime of kites."

"But it sounds rather fishy, if you ask me," added Lali. "Why would a rich buffalo man with piles of money and a crazy love for kites bother, anyway? Oh, and I believe he called you the kite flyer with most promise and potential. At least that's what Ganga said, and Ganga, as everybody knows, is not a liar."

"I guess I should go right away to claim the big prize, huh?" Paki said.

"Oh, don't go on our account," I said. "Ganga might have heard his father wrong. This all sounds too good to be true."

"Hold on!" Paki barked. "If you think you can talk me

out of a pile of money, you are bigger fools than you look!"

"Well then, you should go this minute because the offer expires soon," Lali said. "We'll tag along, just in case Ganga got it all mixed up. If he did, I will give him a good talking to."

Paki dashed away and we followed him, as fast as we could, all the way to the Milk Man's house.

"Where is he?" Paki demanded. "He better be here and he better be on time. I have important things to do."

Ganga came out of the house, wiping his hands on a towel. "I see that Lali told you about my father's prize money. He's w-w-waiting for you in the b-b-buffalo shed and you b-b-better go now b-b-because he is about ready to change his mind."

"I came just as soon as I heard, pal," Paki said. "I would have come sooner if the she-donkeys didn't yakkity-yak so much!"

"Well, b-b-best to go now. He's feeling very generous."

Paki darted into the shed. Lali and I slammed the door shut, and Ganga slipped the bolt in place.

Then we ran away and hid behind a tree. Pretty soon, we heard Paki.

"Hello? There's no one here but the buffalo. Where's the Milk Man?"

In a minute he started banging on the inside of the door. "Hey, what's going on here? Open up!"

# Chapter 27

Lali and I went straightaway to see about Bala and found him fussing over Kalu.

"Let's tell him about Paki, *accha?*" Lali gave my shoulder a nudge.

"*Na!*" I said. "We better not distract him just now."

We eased closer.

"*Oi!* How goes it with you?" I asked.

"Well enough." Bala ran a comb down Kalu's shiny, freshly washed back. "What business is it of yours, *hanh?*"

"We have a 15 percent stake in this show. That makes it our business!" Lali cried.

"We came to see if everything was in shipshape order," I added.

"Scat!" Bala waved his arm. "I'm in charge and I got up with the rooster. Didn't sleep a wink last ni—"

"Never mind all that," I interrupted. "Have you remembered about Kalu's cute hat and the motia garland for his neck? Of course you haven't! This is precisely why we're here, see?"

"You should do something about your wrinkled shirt and that giant mess on your head!" said Lali.

"And when you're done with that, follow us to my hut," I ordered. "Amma has a vermilion dot ready for your forehead. She has made benedictions from her prayer platter for your success."

Drawn by Dev and Hari's drumbeat, the crowds gathered in the field. Lali and I crossed our fingers. With Paki locked in the buffalo shed, the show should go on without a hitch.

When the clock began to strike, Bala strode into the arena like a mighty warrior, Kalu the Wonder Dog trotting at his side.

"Kalu! Kalu! Kalu!" The crowd joined in our chant.

Bala bowed and raised his hand for silence. The crowd hushed and the show began.

"*Aa!*" said Bala, and Kalu came bounding toward him. "Sit!" Bala commanded and Kalu sat. "Spin!" and Kalu spun like a top.

"*Wah!*" cheered the crowd. "More! More!"

And Kalu, the dear dog, did not disappoint! He stood up on his hind legs, lolled his tongue, and begged; he barked on command; he rolled over and played dead. One after another, he masterfully performed the tricks he had worked so hard to learn.

Just before the grand finale, Bala walked Kalu in a circle. Lali and I held our breath; it was time for the great hoop leap. *Would he make it? Wouldn't he?* "Do it, Kalu, do it," we chanted under our breath.

Bala positioned himself, holding the hoop and a bone.

"Lower the hoop a smidgen!" I yelled. I turned to Lali. "I hope he remembers to wave the bone."

Bala bowed to the crowd and raised the hoop. "Come, Kalu!" he called in a voice that was strong and clear.

And Kalu came! He came bounding!

"Go, Kalu!" we shouted. "Jump!"

And Kalu did! He jumped like a champ!

We cheered and clapped and whistled. Kalu had come through with flying colors. He was truly a Wonder Dog!

We counted one hundred thirty-five rupees worth of ticket sales that day.

"What is one half of 15 percent of one hundred thirty-five?" Lali asked me. But before I could tell her, Bala pocketed all the money.

"I'd say that was pretty good amount for a day's work," he crowed. "I'm going to double it in no time at all!"

"Oh ho!" I shouted. "What about our commission, *hanh?*

"What commission?" Bala asked.

It felt like Bapu's cot had given way, spilling me to the ground. Was Bala going back on his word?

And if he was, how did that make him different from me? So many untruths had fallen from my mouth again and again. *Serves you right, liar and word breaker!* I told myself.

I recovered enough to run after Bala and whack him on the shoulder. "*Oi!* Not so fast! We had an agreement! Fifteen percent. Hand it over!"

Bala raised his hands in mock alarm. "*Accha baba!* I was only having a bit of fun with you! I am good for my word."

Lali's smile reached from ear to ear. "Like my dear Ganga, Bala is not one to tell a lie!"

"Fifteen percent of one hun—"

"We should first set Paki free, *accha?*" she said, interrupting my calculations. "Also like my dear Ganga, Bala will keep a promise. This I know in my heart."

Poor Paki! I did feel a little sorry that he was locked up with a bunch of smelly buffalo and smellier piles of hay.

"Fifteen percent and not a smidgen less!" I cried and we ran to rescue Paki. "He's going to be madder than a bull stung on the behind by a bee. There's no telling what he might do!"

Ganga was waiting for us near his house. "The rascal stole my firecrackers, I'll get him for that b-b-before he gets you for the lockup," he said forcefully.

I was so taken aback, I didn't know what to say.

"We'll tiptoe up and unlock the door," Lali said. "By the time he discovers the bolt's open, we'll be a mile away!"

As we approached the buffalo shed, I whispered,

"Remember to run like the wind, Lali. Run like you've never run before!"

But the door to the shed was wide open!

"He got away!" I screamed. "What the—?"

We ran into the shed. Only the buffalo stood there, chewing their straw as if nothing had happened.

Ganga went to check on the rest of his firecrackers. "W-w-why, there are twenty in here."

"All twenty? You said your best and fiercest were gone, *nai?*" I demanded.

"They *were* gone if Ganga said so!" Lali retorted.

"But they're all here!" I said. "How do you explain that?"

"He took them. That much I know from the bulge in the rascal's pocket. But now I'm thinking there was a change of heart and he returned them," Lali said.

"A change of heart? Paki? Rubbish!"

"It *is* possible, is it not?" Lali asked.

"*Humph!*" I snorted.

But it was true. All twenty of Ganga's firecrackers were in the box.

We searched every inch of the shed, but Paki was not there. Where was he?

"I bet he's lurking nearby, waiting to pounce on us!" I said.

We looked for Paki everywhere. Finally, we found him at the water pump, spraying Ramu's goat. As we approached, he turned the spray on us. I noticed from a distance that his pocket was no longer bulging. Perhaps there was truth in Lali's words.

"I have a thing or two to say to you!" he screamed.

"Who let you out?" I asked.

"The Milk Man did, thank you very much!" Paki growled. "He heard me pounding on the door and set me free. And he gave me two eight anna coins! 'Buy a new kite,' the good man said. 'And next year, try a little harder to be champion.'"

"What about the firecrackers, *hanh?*" I asked.

"What firecrackers?" Paki said.

"What firecrackers, he asks?" I turned to Lali in disgust.

"The ones you planned to scare Kalu with!" Lali said.

"I don't know what you fools are blabbering!" Paki rolled his eyes.

"Go! Go!" I protested. "We're not the fools!"

"Paki, you returned them. *Shabaash!* Bravo! It was the right thing to do," Lali said.

Paki grumbled a bit and twirled his finger near his temple like we were crazy, but when he turned back to the goat, I thought I saw a sly little smile at the corner of his mouth.

Then Amma called and Vimla Mausi hallooed and Pentamma Mausi threatened to twist our ears. What could we do? We *had* to go.

# Chapter 28

"Where are you going?" Paki demanded as I went to collect our commission from Bala the next morning.

"To watch Bala practice new tricks with Kalu," I lied. I didn't want the *goonda* boys to know about the commission.

"What? More tricks?" Paki demanded.

"Who does he think he is, Juntar Muntar the Magician?" Raju snickered.

"Get out of my way!" I tried to skirt around them. "You're just jealous he's turning into a businessman!"

But they both pushed up against me, forcing me to take a step back.

"Well, well!" Paki's nose was one inch away from my face. "You *are* sweet on him, aren't you, with your Bala this, and Bala that?"

"You're crazy!" I shoved him away.

"I bet she wants to marry him!" Raju chimed in.

"She may as well," Paki chortled. "She's so ugly, she drips ugliness. And he's so ugly, he oozes ugliness. Their three kids will be named: Ugly, Uglier, and Ugliest!"

I raised my arm to punch him, but he grasped my wrist. When I tried to twist free, he held on tightly.

"*Oi!* Lookee here!" he said, and before I knew it, my ring was in his hand.

"Give it back!" I screamed, but Paki threw the ring to his brother.

"Come and get it, she-donkey!" Raju laughed.

Back and forth the ring traveled, from Paki to Raju, always just a little beyond my reach. They walked as they threw it, passing the beetle nut stand and the seller of bangles.

I jumped and flailed about, but I couldn't catch it. "GIVE MY RING BACK!" I shrieked.

As we neared Lalla-ji's grain shop, the ring whizzed overhead and ricocheted off Raju's hand. I lunged for it. It bounced off the pavement once, *ping...* It bounced again and again...*ping, ping*. Then it rolled into a dark hole—the hole that went all the way to *Inglistan!*

My ring was gone forever! I was too tired to be angry. I just cried and cried until there were no more tears left. When I looked up, Paki and Raju had disappeared.

I told Amma what had happened. She clucked her tongue, but she didn't volunteer to go down the hole to look for the ring and she didn't offer to buy me another one.

"Someone ought to twist their ears, beat them to a pulp, and flay their hides!" I raged.

"Hush, Basanta!" said Amma. "Sister Pentamma will mete out a just punishment."

"Give me a bigger and better ring for my birthday... that's what Pentamma Mausi should do!" I wailed. *"Hanh! That would be just!"*

"You forget something, daughter," Amma said softly. "We all live together in a *busti*. You, as well as they."

"Amma, I wish we had piles and piles of money to get nice things whenever I wanted them," I sniffled.

"You already have what really matters," my mother said.

Old Nahni might have said that too, if she were alive.

"The ring was never truly yours, my daughter," Amma went on. "But this"—she swept out her arm to include herself and Bapu and Durga and everything else inside my little hut—"*this* is truly yours."

I knew my mother was trying to make me feel better, but the pain in my heart was strong.

"*Na*, Amma," I cried. "You are right but also wrong. The ring *was* truly mine. Not at first, but surely later."

"Why do you mourn its loss so?" my mother asked. "You had grown dissatisfied with it of late and talked a great deal about its imperfections."

"Still, I loved it!" I protested. "I loved it as I love Durga despite her annoyances and you despite your scolding."

I sulked and pouted so much Amma sent me to the

water pump to cool off. There, I saw a baby toad hopping and splashing in the cool water. That put a smile on my face and I returned to our hut with a lighter step.

When Bapu got home, he chucked me under the chin and told me he'd buy me a nicer ring for my wedding trousseau. That helped too.

That night, I searched the sky for the star that hid Old Nahni. If she were still alive, I'd run to her, rest my head in her lap, and ask her why I had lost my ring. She would have had some good answers for me—answers I couldn't figure out on my own.

I had a dream in the night. I was digging for gold under the tamarind tree, but I only found slippery seeds. Brown, slippery seeds.

"Where's my gold?" I asked, getting angry.

From above, a voice squawked, "*Caw! Caw!* Basanta has the ring!"

It wasn't Dinoo Kaka. It was Little Bibi.

"Please," I implored. "Not so loudly. My mother will hear!"

Then Amma appeared with a broom in her hand. "Must not forget corners," she muttered. "Must not, must not!"

Finally Old Nahni flew down in the shape of the night owl. She perched on a branch right next to Little Bibi.

"I've lost my gold, Nahni!" I cried. "Tell me where to look!"

The night owl flapped her wings and hooted, "*Hoo Hoo.* Look inside you, silly dear! Look behind the vein that throbs in your neck." Then she flew away upon the night breeze.

"Wait, don't go!" I cried, but she was already just a dot in the sky. I woke up with a start. It was very, very dark and high above me, one star twinkled brighter than the others.

# Chapter 29

O n the day of the *Divali* festival, the *busti* looked like a candle-lit cake. The greenery draped over the doorways of the huts was the icing.

Amma had swept our hut inside and out, and I had arranged all the festive sweets by the hearth. The bright yellow *laddu* that was promised to Bala was among them.

The *diyya* were placed just so, waiting to be lit. Soon they would flicker like fireflies at night.

We dusted off the camphor from our special clothes and I picked out an anklet, a nose-ring, and a necklace from the Big Box. I pulled my *lengha* drawstring snug, made a big crimson dot in the middle of my forehead, and lined my eyes with kohl. Then all prettied up in my newest red and green *Divali* dress, with lovely slippers snug on my feet, I ducked out to show myself off to Lali and walked right into her in the doorway.

"*Oo Maa!* So pretty!" she said, examining my finery up close.

I showed her my book from Little Bibi. "Nice, *nai?* First I will learn to read and then I will teach you."

Lali traced the words with her finger. "Yes, very nice!" She smiled. "I want to know what the words say too."

I sat down and rummaged in my collection box for my shiny mica wafer—the one that Little Bibi had refused. I handed it to Lali.

"*Hanh!*" she squealed. "*This* I like very much!"

"Really? Why?" I asked.

Lali looked at me as though I had lost my mind. "Because," she explained. "Because we can do one hundred things with it, silly!"

I nodded. It was nice that Lali's mind worked like mine. We were two wheels that spun in unison; we never slipped a notch nor missed a beat.

My thumb went to look for the ring that was no longer on my finger. For a minute I had forgotten. It was force of habit, nothing more.

"Your ring!" Lali cried. "Where is it?"

"The *badmaash goonda* boys...." The words started to flow out of my mouth like Bala's kite on a burst of spring wind, but a voice inside said, *Stop, Basanta!* I reeled the words back in, just as Bala reeled in his kite.

"It fell in the drain hole," I said. *Hanh.* Better this way. Better than getting hot and bothered and angry again.

"*Oo Maa!*" Lali cried. "Let's try to get it back!"

"*Na.* It fell deep down in the hole. It's gone forever."

"*Hanh,*" Lali said softly. "Don't be sad. Remember, bad things happen, good things follow."

Lali's words squeezed through my ears and tapped on

my brain. I stared at her. How wise my friend was! How true were her words!

She went on. "My mother does not have enough money for a ring, but she will pray for you. She'll pray for good health and good fortune and also for a very handsome husband for you! That's better than a silly ring, *nai?*"

I shrugged again. I was in no hurry to get married anytime soon.

Lali shifted uncomfortably. "There's something I...."

"What's wrong? Is something the matter?" I asked.

"I am only thinking about the commission."

*Daiyya!* Our 15 percent! I struck my temple with my palm so hard I nearly knocked myself over. "Oh, Lali, I forgot, but now I remember and I will get our share by hook or by crook!"

*Bang, bang, bang!* We heard firecrackers exploding in the field.

"It's Paki and Raju!" I cried, scrambling up. "They're breaking the rules again. They're starting before the sun is properly set!"

Lali and I hurried toward our huts to get our sparklers.

# Chapter 30

"O i!" Ramu called to me. "Where's the fire, little one?" He and Rukmani were holding hands under the mango tree.

"Hiding in my sparklers," I yelled. "And we're going for them right now!"

I wanted to stay and tease him. *Aha! Holding hands in broad daylight, hanh?* But Paki and Raju were already in the field, and the acrid smell of sulphur was heavy in the air.

"Don't you want to stop and look at what I have?" Rukmani called.

Lali and I exchanged knowing looks. I knew we were thinking the same thing: *Oh ho...Miss Nimblefingers!*

"Come here, and I'll tell you about *my* sparkler," said Rukmani.

It was the sweetness in her voice that made us stop. Rukmani sounded so unlike her usual rude self.

"Well, tell us!" I said. "*Juldi, juldi!* Quickly, quickly!"

Rukmani pointed her chin at Ramu. "He bought these nice sparklers for me," she said, batting her eyes at him. What happened to the spitfire? Where was the acid tongue? Where did the snarls go?

Ramu grinned from ear to ear; he looked like Kalu begging for a bone. That dear man, he positively glowed. Rukmani and Ramu...why, the sound of their names together was not so bad, after all!

"There's something else." Ramu spoke so quietly we almost didn't hear.

"Yes, Ramu?" I tapped my foot on the ground. *Tick, tick, tick,* time was passing and the *goonda* boys' firecrackers were getting louder by the minute.

"She took them back," Ramu said softly.

"What did she take back, *hanh?*"

"The black beads. And the chickens," he said. "She took them back to her *memsaab's* yard where they belong."

Rukmani stood by his side, tracing arcs in the dirt with her big toe.

*Oo Ma!* It looked like there might be a real wedding in the *busti* before the next mango harvest. *Shabaash,* Ramu! Well done! I'd thread a nice motia garland for his darling's glossy black hair. I would!

"There you are." Amma smiled at me. "Look who just got here."

Bala sat on his haunches, eating *laddu* near Amma's stove. He hadn't forgotten the *Divali laddu* after all, and he had likely not forgotten the sparklers Amma had promised him either.

I went to my treasure box and picked out two for him. "These are for you and I expect to get back sevenfold!" I said.

Bala's licked yellow crumbs from the side of his mouth and wiped his hands down his sides. "What's she talking about, Yella Mausi?" he asked my mother.

"She's already got it back, and more," Amma said. "She just doesn't know it yet."

"I have? I don't see seven times two sparklers in my box. I see only eight, which is ten minus the two I just gave away."

"Silly child!" chided Amma gently. "I'm talking about dear Bala's present and future success. Isn't that worth more?"

"My next Wonder Dog Show is coming along," Bala said, "but there are some problems."

"Do not worry. I'll come by after *Divali* and we can talk about it," I told him.

Amma smiled at us. "What will you do with all the coins you will earn, dear boy?" she asked him.

"I will add them to the cash prize from the good Milk Man. I will buy boxes of black and brown boot polish and set up a stand near Lalla-ji's store and yell, *Boot Paalish! Boot Paalish!*"

"*Shabaash!* Bravo!"

"And with the money from that I'll buy chickens and with the eggs—"

"One step at a time, dear boy," Amma said. "One small step at a time."

With a wave of his hand, Bala jumped up like a *gilli* hit by a *danda* stick. He sped away, whooping and leaping in the fading light.

"Wait! What about my commission?" I yelled, but he was already gone.

"What commission?" my mother asked.

"From the dog show," I replied. "We earned it; Lali and I helped from start to finish!"

"You mean the twenty rupees and twenty-five paisa he brought for you today?"

"He did? Where is it?" I held out my palm.

"I gave it back to him," my mother said matter-of-factly. "He needs it more than you do."

I couldn't believe Amma had returned our money without asking. "I worked hard for it, Amma," I cried. "I truly did!"

"You earned far more than that, daughter," Bapu said. "You've earned his lasting friendship."

"You d-don't understand," I stammered. "Half of it belongs to Lali."

At the mention of Lali, Amma's voice softened. "Lali had a share in this? You keep many secrets from me, daughter."

"I am sorry for so much, Amma. I truly am. Please, let me have my commission and...and...I'll give it all to Lali! I will!"

"Let Bala have his money, child," Amma said. Then she untied the money knot in her *pullo* and counted out eleven rupee notes, one by one. "Give this to Lali."

"What about my share?" I asked.

"You shall have yours too, by and by," Amma said. Then she folded me in her arms. "But I will tell you this, daughter: next time come to me first, before you take so much upon yourself."

"I will, Amma," I cried. "God promise!" I pinched my throat so hard it bruised my skin.

Then I rummaged in my treasure box for my stash of sparklers. "I'll go to Bala tomorrow, Amma, to help him plan his boot *paalish* business," I said as I ducked out the doorway of my hut. "I am in a big hurry to go to the field just now. You see, Paki and Raju have started without us. Rascals!"

I ran for Lali and found Vimla Mausi working a grind-stone near her hut. *Zum-zup, zum-zup,* sang stone on stone.

"Basanta!" she cried, raining down a shower of wheat grain from her fist. "We will eat roti cooked in pure ghee tonight!"

Payday had arrived in time for the Festival of Lights, and the worry lines had been swept away from Mausi's brow at last.

"*Mmm.* Amma's always making piping hot roti for Little Bibi's breakfast! It's so flaky and buttery it makes me drool! " I licked my lips. "It'll be a proper *Divali* feast in your home too, *nai?*"

Mausi beamed. *"Hanh*, dear child. It surely will."

"Where's Lali?" I asked. Except for Mausi and the grinding stone, the hut was silent.

"She's just run off to the field with the little ones," Vimla Mausi replied. Glass bangles tinkled on her wrist and the pocked stone spun merrily round and round and round.

*Oo!* That Lali! She didn't even wait for me!

*Boom! Crack! Bang!*

*Rat-tat-tat!*

*Whizzzzz!*

The fiery showers, the exploding firecrackers, and the happy squeals of my friends beckoned from the field. I held my sparklers tightly in one hand, hitched up my *lengha* above my ankles with the other, and I ran to them.

# Glossary

*Child of Spring* is set in the state of Hyderabad in India. Today it is the joint capital of Andhra State and Telangana. Prior to 1948, Hyderabad was the largest princely state in India, and Urdu was the official language. Then it was forcibly annexed into the Indian federation, and in 1956, it became part of the state of Andhra Pradesh. Telugu is the official language of Andhra Pradesh. Other languages spoken in the region include Hindi, Tamil, Kannada, and Odia.

Most of the foreign words and phrases in this story are in Hindi, with one exception, noted below.

*aa*: a beckoning call, to signal someone to come
*accha*: "Okay"
*accha baba*: "All right"
*accha-ji*: "Yes sir/madam" (said with respect)
*aiyyo*: "Oh dear!" or "Oh no!" (Tamil, usually used by females)
*almarah*: wardrobe
*amma*: mother
*Angrezi*: English
anna: Indian currency, equal to 1/16 rupee

*arrey baba*: "Oh, man!"

*arrey daiyya*: "Oh dear!"; "Dear me!"; or "Oh my!" (usually used by females)

*arrey wah*: "Oh wow!"

*arri*: "Hey you" (when addressing a female.)

*baap re*: "Oh my gosh!"

*baba*: literally means father, though a small child may also be called *baba*. At times, *baba* is inserted in conversation without any real meaning, as in *arrey baba* ("Oh, man!") or *na baba* ("No way!")

*badmaash*: naughty

*bapu*: father

*bas*: "Enough of that!"

*beedi*: a type of cigarette made with unprocessed tobacco rolled in a leaf

*bhangra*: a traditional folk dance originating in the Punjab region

*bindi*: a red dot on the center of the forehead, commonly worn by Hindu women

*Bo Kata*: loosely translated, it means 'Hacked!" Used as a victory cry during kite fights.

*busti*: a small community of huts

*chappati*: unleavened flatbread, also known as roti

*charpai*: a traditional bed, consisting of a set of woven ropes within a wooden frame. The user lies directly on the ropes without a mattress.

*chi*: "For shame!"

*choli*: a short, blouse that reveals the midriff; the upper
  garment for a sari

*chullah*: a stove used to cook food over a fire

*chup*: "Be quiet!"

*churan*: a sweet and sour digestive powder

*dhal:* a thick or runny stew prepared from lentils. A staple
  in South Asian cuisine.

*daiyya*: god

*daiyaa re daiyya*: " Oh god!"

*Divali*: the Festival of Lights, a Hindu festival celebrated in
  India during October or November

*diyya*: a small, oil burning lamp

dhoti: a loincloth worn by men

ghee: clarified butter

*gilli danda*: an amateur sport, using two small pieces of
  wood, played in rural areas through the Indian
  subcontinent. It is believed to be the origin of games
  like cricket, baseball, and softball.

*goonda*: stupid person

*hanh*: yes

*hutt*: "Out of the way!"

*hulla goolla*: hullaballoo

*Inglistan*: England

*ji*: an honorific suffix  intended to convey respect to the
  individual to whose name it is appended

*juldi*: "Hurry!"

*katori*: a small bowl

# Child of Spring

kurta: a loose shirt, falling to just above or below the knee,
worn by men and women

*laddu*: a ball-shaped sweet, popular in the Indian
Subcontinent, made of flour, minced dough, sugar, and
other ingredients

*lengha*: a long, embroidered, and pleated skirt that is
worn with a *choli* as a style of sari

maharani: empress

*manja*: thread, coated with powdered glass, used in kite
fights

*mausi*: aunty (mother's sister). In India and Pakistan, non-
blood relatives are routinely addressed as aunt, uncle,
grandfather, grandmother, etc.

*memsaab*: a title used for a woman of authority

*na*: "No"

*na baba*: "No way"

*nai*: Yes?

*oi*: "hey you!"

*oo maa*: "Oh dear!" or "Oh my!" (usually used by females)

paisa: Indian currency. 100 paisa=1 rupee.

*pullo*: the long trailing part of a sari, worn draped around
or across the shoulders

*Ram Ram*: a respectful greeting in North India, in which
the name of the Hindu deity Ram is repeated two
times, often with folded palms

*rangoli*: folk art created on the floor using colored rice, dry
flour, or colored sand; it is usually made during *Divali*

rani: queen
roti: Indian flat bread
rupee: Indian currency. 100 paise=1 rupee
sadhu: a religious ascetic or holy person
sari: a garment draped around the body, traditionallyworn
    by women
sahib: a polite title for a man
*ser*: a unit of mass measure equivalent to approximately
    2.5 pounds
*shabaash*: "Bravo!"
*shor*: noise
*tamasha*: a spectacle
*thaana*: police station
*thali*: a sectioned platter that holds a variety of dishes
*theek thack*: shipshape
*ub*: now
wallah: a person associated with a specific business or
    type of work